SCENT OF MURDER

A CHRISTIAN ROMANTIC SUSPENSE

SULLIVAN K9 SEARCH AND RESCUE
BOOK 9

LAURA SCOTT

PROLOGUE

Helen Gingrass took her dying patient's hand in hers. Stuart Ramsey was about the same age as her son, which made his imminent demise from stage four cancer difficult to bear.

"I need the chaplain." Stuart's voice was raspy. He stared up at her with eyes that weren't quite focused. "I need to confess my sins."

"The chaplain is on his way." Helen offered a reassuring smile. As a nurse for forty years, she'd heard a few confessions in her time. Mostly about infidelity.

"He needs to hurry." Stuart's eyes slid closed, then popped open again. "I don't have much time. I can't die with this crime on my conscience."

Crime? Helen frowned. That was a first. "He's

with another patient. He'll be here as soon as he can get away."

"I need to confess!" Stuart's voice held urgency. His fingers tightened on hers, and he let out a hacking cough. "I sabotaged a plane six years ago. I caused the deaths of three people. Only I didn't know there would be three people."

She was having trouble following his confession. "You didn't intend to kill anyone, right?"

He grimaced. "I was paid to kill the pilot. That's all. I took care of the plane, I used to be a mechanic, and I took care of the plane." He swallowed hard. "But I didn't know there would be two other people on board." His breathing grew agitated. "I didn't know!"

"Easy, Stuart, try to relax." Helen did her best to reassure him, despite the shocking statement he'd just made. He'd purposefully sabotaged a plane to kill the pilot! She needed to call the police. Maybe even the FBI.

"I didn't know the pilot had a son. Dominic Lakeland. I ruined so many lives." He lifted his tortured gaze to hers. "I need . . . God to forgive me . . ." His voice trailed off. Then he let out another wet cough as his eyes closed. Helen frowned. She wasn't a chaplain, so she wasn't sure that simply confessing his sins was good enough.

"Do you regret what you did? Do you repent

your sins?" She wished the chaplain would hurry up and get there. Despite working hospice for the past few years, she wasn't accustomed to taking deathbed confessions of this magnitude. And she had no idea how to guide this man spiritually. In her mind, murder was a pretty big sin.

"Yes. I needed the money . . . but I know that's not an excuse." He abruptly pulled away to rummage in the pocket of his hoodie. In hospice, patients could wear whatever made them comfortable. He pulled out something that was small and round. "Take this." He pushed it into her hand. "I don't have any family, and it's all I have left. Take it."

"Oh, I can't." Nurses weren't allowed to take money or gifts from their patients. That was against their code of ethics.

"Please, take it. Worth . . ." His voice trailed off as his breath rattled in his throat. His eyes closed.

Then he stopped breathing altogether. His hand went limp, and his head lolled to the side.

Helen pulled free, staring down at the coin he'd given her. It didn't look real; it certainly wasn't any currency she recognized. It was gold in color and had the picture of a man's face on the front. Rearranging her bifocals on her nose, she could make out the words South Africa along the side. Was this a South African rand? Maybe Stuart had meant to say it was worthless. If it was worthless, it wouldn't be against the rules to take it.

Still, Helen felt uneasy as she pocketed the coin. She'd have to take it somewhere to be appraised. If it was worth money, she could take the funds and donate them to the hospice center. Satisfied with that approach, she stepped back from the bedside and made a note of the time of death.

With that task finished, she decided to call the police. And this Dominic Lakeland whose father was killed. Stuart had confessed to a crime.

Everyone, especially the man's son, needed to know the truth.

1

Dominic Lakeland slowed his speed as he caught sight of the Redwood Motel, the place Kendra Sullivan had suggested he stay while in Greybull. The recent news he'd learned about his father's plane crash had circled around in his brain during the long drive from Billings, Montana. What should have been a two-hour ride had turned out to be three and a half, thanks to the recent snowfall. Not only had it caused traffic to slow to a crawl, but he'd had to get out and help a stranded mother of two who'd gotten herself stuck in a high snowbank along the side of the road.

Dom wanted nothing more than to get out and stretch his legs. Even driving his large Ford truck, his six-foot-seven-inch frame had made him feel like a pretzel behind the wheel.

Now that he was in Wyoming, though, he was anxious to meet Kendra face-to-face. She'd reached out two months ago asking him if he knew anything about the plane crash that had killed his father, who was the pilot, and her parents, the passengers. At the time, he'd only known as much as she did. When Kendra had mentioned her sister's cadaver dog, Denali, had found skeletal remains from his father, he'd been intrigued. He and Kendra had been communicating mostly through email and text messages, along with one computer video call when she'd encouraged him to drive down so they could discuss what might have happened. Kendra had never believed the plane crash six years ago was an accident.

Turns out, Kendra was right. When the hospice nurse had called a week ago to let him know her patient had confessed to murdering his father, he'd been stunned. She'd called the police, too, and the very next day, the Billings police had contacted him about the news. He'd asked what the plan was moving forward, but the cops had simply shrugged. The guy had confessed, and that was that. Case closed.

It wasn't case closed for him and Kendra, though. He burned with the need to know why his dad had been killed. He and Kendra had arranged to dig further into Stuart Ramsey to find out more. He'd agreed to drive down to Greybull, but now that he was seeing the Redwood Motel in person, he had second thoughts about the plan.

It was too late to turn back now. Glancing at the clock, he slowed and pulled into the parking lot of the motel. Then he headed around toward the back of the property. It was going on five o'clock in the afternoon—probably too late for them to get together that evening, but they could meet for breakfast. He put the gearshift into park and sent Kendra a quick text, letting her know he'd made it to the motel. Then he killed the engine.

As he slid out from behind the wheel of his Ford truck, he caught a hint of movement from the corner of his eye. He turned to get a better look just as the sound of gunfire split the night.

What in the world? He ducked and pressed himself against the metal frame of the truck, fighting to stay calm. Fear washed over him as he crab-walked around the front of the vehicle, trying to figure out where the shooter was located. It wasn't easy to see in the dark, despite his new contact lenses. Vanity had him trading his glasses for contacts, even though he wasn't quite used to wearing them. Stupid of him to want to look better for Kendra.

Another crack of gunfire had him lowering his

head even farther. His heart slammed against his sternum as adrenaline raced through his bloodstream. It didn't make any sense that someone would be gunning for him. His life was boring. Predictable. He didn't even live in Wyoming. Who was out there? A crazy hunter? Someone else? Had he interrupted some other crime in progress?

Maybe this was related to his father's murder? How, he wasn't sure. Even the cops had considered it case closed. He swallowed hard, realizing that staying put wasn't an option. Not if the gunman intended to keep shooting. Unless the guy had already taken off? Dom eased up to peer around the edge of his truck.

Another crack of gunfire rang out. He ducked again, blinking to clear his vision. At twenty-eight years old, he'd never once been targeted by gunfire. Would someone inside the motel call the police? Did Greybull have a police department, or would he have to wait for a sheriff's deputy to arrive?

Another bullet pinged off the hood of his truck, far too close to his head. He was really starting to get ticked off. Where was this guy? And why was he shooting at him?

Since he couldn't see where the shooter was hiding, Dom decided to make a run for it. He darted into the woods, keeping his head down. The foliage provided decent cover, especially the large pine trees. He was grateful for that until he glanced back over his shoulder and realized he was leaving boot prints in the snow.

Not good. This was not good! Picking up the pace, he ran through the trees. After several yards, he made a wide circle to double back. There had to be a way to get a look at this guy who'd fired so many shots at his truck. Maybe this was a case of mistaken identity?

No, that didn't make sense. The shooter should have noticed his Montana license plates. He swallowed hard, realizing this must have been related to his father's murder. Why anyone would come after him six years after the fact, he had no idea. Especially since Stuart Ramsey confessed to the crime.

Maybe he and Kendra were right not to consider the case closed.

Taking a quick break, he crouched behind an evergreen, straining to listen. After hearing so many gunshots, the ensuing silence was eerie. He drew in a deep breath to calm his racing heart. Had the shooter given up and left? Or had the guy headed into the woods to find him?

What if there was more than one of them? A band of fear tightened around his chest. He was about to pull out his phone to dial 911 when he heard a rustling sound.

An animal? Or human? Probably the latter.

Giving up the idea of making a call, which would have given away his location, he eased farther into the woods. He glanced over his shoulder, wincing when he again saw his tracks.

They were so obvious a blind man could have followed them.

It couldn't be helped. Continuing in a half circle, he gauged where the road was located. Maybe a half mile? If he could reach the road, he knew the hard-packed snow that had been flattened by numerous tire tracks would help cover his footprints. He could take the road for a while before heading back into the woods. When he was safe, he could call 911.

Dom continued moving swiftly through the forest. Pausing near a large oak tree, he thought he saw movement. With a frown, he ducked and scanned the woods. For long moments, he didn't move, barely breathing as he watched and listened.

There! A dark shadow stepped out from behind a tree. Dom could see the guy held a handgun. Swallowing hard, he stayed put, hoping the guy would turn away.

He didn't. Instead, another crack of gunfire reverberated through the woods.

Enough already! Dom spun and ran, doing a zigzag pattern from one tree to the next. His long legs worked to his advantage now, and while he'd never run for pleasure, he didn't let that slow him down.

Where were the local cops? Hadn't anyone from the motel called them?

Dom continued in the general direction of the road. After what seemed like eons, he caught a glimpse of the plowed street through a break in the trees. He slowed his pace, fearing there could be a second man out there waiting for him to emerge. Hunkering down beside a tree, he waited. Headlights indicated a car was moving down the street from the west. He waited until it had passed, then rushed out to the road.

Seeing nobody lurking nearby, he broke into a jog, running west, away from the hotel. Glancing over his shoulder, he was relieved to see his footprints weren't readily visible on the hard-packed snow. With renewed energy, he picked up his speed, putting even more distance between himself and the shooter.

After traveling about a mile or so, he noticed another pair of headlights illuminating the sky behind him. The sharp curve in the road made it impossible for him to see what sort of car was approaching. Fearing the gunman had figured out his ploy, he abruptly leaped over the snowbank to get off the road, quickly diving back into the safety of the woods.

Dom kept moving, determined to stay well ahead of the gunman. When he came across a fallen log, he jumped over that, the way he'd hurdled the snowbank. Only this time, he landed at an awkward angle. His right foot slipped, and he lost his balance. Falling, the back of his head struck the fallen tree trunk.

Then there was nothing but darkness.

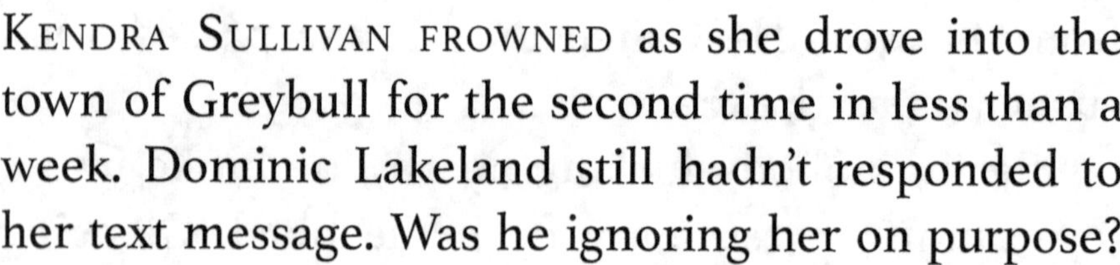

Kendra Sullivan frowned as she drove into the town of Greybull for the second time in less than a week. Dominic Lakeland still hadn't responded to her text message. Was he ignoring her on purpose? That would be strange since he was the one who'd texted her to say he'd arrived at the Redwood Motel.

"What do you think, Smoky?" She eyed her Alaskan malamute in the rearview mirror. "Maybe he brought his girlfriend along and is distracted by spending time alone with her."

Smoky gave a halfhearted wag of her curved tail. Kendra grimaced and turned her attention to the road. She didn't care if Dominic brought his girlfriend along for the ride or not. She was anxious to talk to him. The news of Stuart Ramsey's confession filled her with a renewed sense of purpose. For years, she'd suspected foul play related to the deaths of her parents. Now they knew the truth. But they still didn't know why. What possible motive could there have been to kill Dominic's father? Hopefully, she and Dominic could piece the puzzle together before Christmas.

She hadn't told her eight older siblings the recent revelation about the murder or her plan to meet Dominic. For one thing, they treated her as if she was still a kid, not a twenty-five-year-old woman. And for another, they'd take over the investigation. Maybe she was being silly, but since they hadn't taken her seriously six years ago, she was determined to uncover the truth herself.

She slowed her speed. If she remembered right, the motel was a mile past the sharp curve.

A pickup truck barreled around the hairpin curve, going much faster than the posted speed limit. Thankfully, she was hugging the right side of the street and wasn't hit. Kendra followed the dark truck with her gaze, then sighed and shook her head. Some people just didn't care about how their reckless driving impacted others.

Moments later, she saw the sign for the Redwood Motel. She slowed to pull into the parking lot, then frowned when she saw a large silver truck parked off to the back of the lot. It wasn't just the truck that drew her gaze, but the bullet hole in the rear window.

Glancing around, she didn't see any police nearby. She wasn't sure whether the bullet hole was made recently or whether the owner of the truck hadn't bothered to have it fixed.

That's when she noticed the Montana plates. Wait, this was Dominic's truck? She pulled up beside the vehicle, shifted into park, and killed the engine. She released the back hatch for Smoky and pushed out from behind the wheel.

"Dominic? It's Kendra. Are you out here?"

At the sound of her voice, Smoky ran over to her side. Kendra noticed there were several overlapping footprints in the snow around her feet.

"Dominic?" She scanned the area, then noticed Smoky had trotted away from her. She turned to call her K9 when the dog buried her snout in the snow, sniffing intently. Then she sat and let out a sharp bark.

Her alert! Although Kendra hadn't told her to search, the dog had found something of interest.

"What is it, girl?" Kendra hurried over. "What did you find?"

Spying the glint of brass, she bent and picked the shell casing up with her gloved hands. The Sullivan K9s mostly tracked people, but they were cross-trained to find gunpowder, gun oil, and shell casings. Like this. Glancing again at the damaged truck, she wondered if the gunfire had been recent.

And if so, the shell casing was evidence that would need to get to the state crime lab.

Spinning away from the truck, she dropped the shell casing into her pocket and hurried into the motel. Smoky loped at her side. A teenager sat behind the desk with AirPods in his ears, watching a movie on his phone. He didn't so much as glance up when she came inside, and she had to wave her hand in front of his screen to get his attention.

He frowned and plucked an earbud from his ear. "Yeah?"

"Did you hear gunfire?"

"No." He gave her an annoyed look. "Why?"

She barely refrained from rolling her eyes. "I'm here to see Dominic Lakeland. Is he here?"

"Nobody has checked in for the past couple of hours." The clerk glanced down at his phone, then back up at her. "Anything else?"

It was all she could do not to snatch the phone from his hands. "Will you please see if Dominic Lakeland has checked in at all today?"

Heaving a sigh, he turned and tapped keys on the computer. "Nope."

"Thanks." She turned away, her thoughts racing. Where was Dominic? The truck with the Montana plates had to be his. "Come, Smoky."

Back outside, she approached the truck. It was empty except for an overnight case on the floor of the back seat. Seeing another bullet graze grooved into the truck's hood, she grew more concerned. Then she noticed the footprints heading into the woods.

Rather than following the footprints, she went back to her SUV and opened the back hatch. Filling a collapsible bowl with water, she set it down for Smoky. While the dog drank, she shouldered her backpack. When Smoky finished with the water, she tucked the collapsible bowl in the pack, then slammed the hatch shut.

"Here, Smoky." She crossed to the truck and wrenched open the driver's side door. "This is Dominic." She patted the driver's seat. "Dominic. Are you ready to search? Huh, girl? Search Dominic!"

Smoky loved playing the search game. Her K9 pressed her nose into the seat cushion, then sniffed along the floorboard where the gas and brake pedals were located. Shoes and socks were always good scent sources. Then Smoky lifted her snout to the air. Whirling away from the truck, her K9 bounded toward the woods, her curly tail wagging from side to side.

Kendra slammed the truck door shut and quickened her pace to keep up. Smoky bounded along the deep footprints in the snow, using her nose to follow Dominic's path. At some point, another pair of tracks crossed his, making Kendra glad she'd taken the time to provide Smoky with a scent source. The last thing she wanted to do was follow the wrong set of footprints.

Her K9 continued following Dominic's scent. The prints seemed to make a wide circle, leading back to the road. When they finally reached it, Smoky turned right and headed west, still following a scent trail only the dog could find.

"Search Dominic," she called encouragingly. The malamute was at home in the wintery weather. Her K9's thick fluffy coat kept her warm. "Search!"

Smoky trotted down the road. They walked for over a mile or so when her K9 slowed to a stop, sniffing intently at the north side of the street. Then Smoky sat and let out a sharp bark.

"Good girl!" Kendra didn't pull the stuffed hippo from her backpack. "Good girl, Smoky. Search! Search Dominic!"

The dog stared at her for a moment, as if disappointed not to be rewarded, then jumped up to continue. Rather than continuing down the road, the dog turned to head into the woods.

Once again, Kendra saw familiar boot prints in the snow. She tried to imagine why Dominic had come this way. Had the gunman pursued him through the woods? And if so, why had that person taken shots at him in the first place?

Was this related to their parents' murder? She

couldn't see a connection, but then again, it seemed like a strange coincidence that the recent danger wasn't related to the past.

Troubled, she continued following Smoky through the woods. Had Dominic been followed all the way from Billings? Could Dominic be involved in something else? She had not met him in person, although their last conversation had been a face-to-face video call. Dominic was a couple of years older than she was and had short blond hair. He was tall and thin, mentioning wryly that his nickname as a kid had been "beanpole."

He seemed nice enough. But now that she was tracking him through the woods, she found herself wondering if she'd made a mistake coming here. Her oldest brother, Chase, would be angry to know she'd set off to meet with a man she didn't know. Especially the son of a man who'd been murdered, taking their parents down with him.

Smoky sniffed at the base of a tree, then continued moving deeper into the forest. Kendra glanced at her compass, making a mental note of the coordinates. She'd need to make sure she could find her way out of there when she'd located Dominic.

Had he gotten lost? It was easy to get turned around in the forest, especially at night. Not that the hour was that late, only 5:45 in the evening.

Smoky put on a burst of speed, running toward a fallen tree. Her K9 gracefully leaped over the dead tree, landing nimbly on the other side. She lost sight of the dog but heard the sharp bark of her alert.

"What is it, girl? What did you find?" Kendra hurried forward, breathing heavily.

"You're a pretty dog," a low, husky voice said.

She slowed her pace, approaching with caution. She had a handgun in her backpack; they always were armed on SAR missions, mostly due to the threat of wildlife. But there were times when human threats were a problem too. She should have taken the time to slip the .38 into her coat pocket. Taking a few steps closer, she frowned when she saw a man sitting on the ground, his back up against the downed tree.

"Dominic? Dominic Lakeland?" She climbed over the horizontal tree trunk, eyeing him warily. Peering through the darkness, he appeared to be the same man she'd chatted with via the computer. "What happened? Are you okay?"

"Other than being a klutz, yeah. I'm fine." He put a hand to his head, then pushed himself upward. Moving slowly, he turned to face her. "Hey, Kendra. Nice to meet you in person, although I'm sorry it's under these circumstances. Oh, I meant to tell you this before, my friends call me Dom."

"What happened?" She shrugged out of the

backpack and found the stuffed hippo. She tossed it into the air for Smoky, who leaped joyously up to grab it. Her dog loved that goofy hippo, and the K9 proceeded to prance around with the toy in her mouth.

"I slipped and hit my head on the tree trunk." He looked embarrassed as he palpated the back of his head. "I don't think the skin is broken. Thankfully, I have a hard head. I was sitting here getting ready to head back to the motel when your dog leaped down beside me. I recognized Smoky from our screen meeting."

"I meant what happened that you're way out here?" Kendra tipped her head to the side, regarding him thoughtfully. Seeing him on the computer screen hadn't prepared her for just how tall he was. Easily six and a half feet, maybe more. Taller than any of her six older brothers, which was saying something. "I went to the motel and found your bullet-ridden truck. I checked with the kid behind the desk, he was watching some movie on his phone with earbuds in, but he said you hadn't checked in. I sent Smoky out to follow your scent trail. You're fortunate she was able to find you."

"I know you mentioned your K9s are trained in search and rescue, but seeing her in action is amazing." He grimaced. "Sorry to cause trouble. When the bullets started flying, I headed into the woods.

When the gunman followed, I decided to double back to the road to avoid leaving footprints in the snow. I feared that was making it too easy for him to find me."

"Okay, but why is someone shooting at you in the first place?" She gave him a stern look. "What's going on?"

"How should I know?" He frowned. "I was heading into the motel when I saw movement. Suddenly gunfire rings out, forcing me to duck and run for cover. I'm not a criminal, if that's what you're asking. I assume this is related to our parents in some way."

Kendra hesitated, wondering how much she should trust him. Just because they'd texted and emailed and even met on a computer call didn't mean she knew Dom on a personal level. Granted, she was the one who'd reached out to him the moment she'd realized his father, Gary Lakeland, was the pilot of the charter plane her parents were in when it crashed six years ago.

Then he'd called her with the news of Stuart Ramsey's confession. From there, they'd agreed to this meeting.

"If you're in some kind of trouble, Dom, you may as well tell me. I have family members in law enforcement, and I'm sure they could work something out to help you."

"Me? I didn't do anything other than drive down here to talk to you." Annoyance flashed in his eyes. "You're the one who suggested I stay at the Redwood Motel, remember? You're the one who wanted to meet in person to dig into why Stuart Ramsey had been paid to kill my father."

She sighed. He was right. She had been the one to recommend Greybull, the Redwood Motel, and meeting in person to dig into the six-year-old crime. Her last SAR mission involving a lost woman had been in Greybull just a few days earlier, so it seemed appropriate to meet there. "Were you followed from Billings?"

"Not that I noticed." He sighed. "I helped a young mother with two small kids get her SUV out of a snowbank about ten miles outside of Billings. I think I'd have noticed if someone had pulled over and waited for me to hit the road again to follow me here."

A nice gesture on his part. Helping a young mother of two kids made her feel a little better about him. Yet the gunfire at the motel was unnerving. So much so that she knew they couldn't stay there moving forward.

With a sigh, she turned to Smoky. "Here, girl. Hand."

Her K9 trotted forward and dropped the stuffed hippo into the palm of her hand.

"Good girl." She tucked it away, then turned to Dominic. "Let's get out of here."

"I'm in agreement with that plan." He brushed the snow from his clothes, then carefully stepped over the fallen log. She did the same, giving Smoky the hand signal to come. He glanced at her as they retraced their steps. "Thanks for coming out to find me."

"That's what we do." She waved a gloved hand at their surroundings. "I've done searches like this dozens of times over the past few years."

Dom hunched his shoulders. "I feel like an idiot that you had to find me. I don't suppose you saw anyone hanging around the motel? Anyone who might be the shooter?"

She thought about the dark truck that had careened around the hairpin curve in the road, nearly striking her SUV. Was the man driving the truck the same gunman who'd tracked Dominic through the woods?

And if so, why? Why would anyone want Dominic dead six years after his father's murder?

2

As if having to be rescued by Kendra and her K9, Smoky, wasn't bad enough, Dom hated knowing he'd dragged her squarely into danger. Not that he could have anticipated anyone shooting at him. It wasn't as if he knew anything more than he had before.

Except for what the nurse, Helen, had told him about Stuart Ramsey's confession.

Yet now that they were back at the motel, seeing the bullet holes in his truck, it was impossible to ignore the fact that someone wanted him dead.

Stopping behind his truck, he turned to face Kendra. "We need to call the police, then I'll drive back to Billings while you head back to your family's ranch."

She frowned. "I'm okay with calling the police,

but you can't head back to Billings. The shooter might find you there."

"That's my problem, not yours." Kendra was prettier in person with her dark hair and sparkling blue eyes. Not that it should matter one way or the other. She was the innocent victim in this. Just like her parents had been killed simply because they'd been in his father's plane. "I'll handle it."

She scowled. "That's ridiculous. This guy knows what you're driving. Get into my SUV. I'll take you to a new hotel. Somewhere you won't be found."

"Shouldn't we wait here for the cops to arrive?"

"No. Call them on the way. This guy might come back."

He hesitated, wishing there was another option. Greybull was a much smaller town than Billings. He doubted they had rideshare services, so maybe getting a ride from Kendra wasn't the worst idea. "Okay, but after you drop me off, you need to head home. I don't want you to get caught in the cross fire."

"We'll talk to the police and go from there." She used her key fob to unlock the SUV and to open the back hatch. "Up, Smoky."

The beautiful furry dog gracefully leaped into the back crate area. Kendra threw her backpack inside and lowered the hatch as he pulled his overnight case from his truck. He tossed it onto the floor of the back seat, then folded himself into the passenger seat. He moved the seat back to give himself as much leg room as possible.

Kendra slid in beside him, started the car, and pulled out onto the road. "There are more hotel options in Cody."

"That's fine." He didn't like leaving his truck behind, but he wasn't even sure it would run. "Does Greybull have a police department, or will I get patched through to the county sheriff's office?"

"Greybull has a small police force." She offered a lopsided smile. "Smaller than Cody's, which isn't very big either. They get a lot of help from the highway patrol."

"Whatever works." He dialed 911 and waited for the dispatcher to answer.

"911, what is your address?" a female voice asked.

"Um, I'm not sure of the exact address, but I was involved in a shooting incident outside the Redwood Motel about an hour ago. A person fired at me three times until I ran into the woods to escape."

"What's your name, sir?" she asked.

Dom hesitated, then realized they could run his plate to identify him. "Dominic Lakeland. I live in Billings, Montana, and drove down to visit a friend. I planned to stay at the Redwood Motel."

"And you say there was a shooting? Is anyone hurt?"

"Nobody is hurt as far as I know, but my truck is

in the parking lot sporting a couple of bullet holes." He remembered what Kendra said about the clerk wearing earbuds and watching a movie on his phone. No wonder the police hadn't been called. "I think the gunman took off."

"And where are you now, sir?" the dispatcher asked.

"Not at the motel." He realized this call wouldn't be of any help. By the time the officer responded, all he or she would see was a damaged truck. "I'll give you my cell number. The responding officer can call me if he needs more information."

"I have your cell number up on my screen, sir," the dispatcher said. "But I know the responding officer will want to speak with you in person."

"Sorry, that's not happening." He abruptly ended the call, tucking his phone back into his coat pocket. "I think that was a waste of time."

"The incident needs to be put on record." Kendra shrugged. "I'll call my brother-in-law Griff Flannery. He's with the FBI."

He shot her a surprised look. "Seriously?"

"Yep. Another brother-in-law, Doug Bridges, is with the DEA. My oldest sister, Maya, is a former cop too." She arched a brow. "If you are involved in something criminal, my family will figure it out."

"I'm not a criminal!" The words came out

harsher than he had intended. "I didn't do anything to warrant being used for target practice."

"Okay, but you can't blame me for asking." She paused, then asked, "Tell me again what the hospice nurse said. How exactly did she hear Stuart Ramsey's confession?"

He blew out a breath, glad to move on to the real reason they were there together. "The nurse's name is Helen Gingrass. Stuart Ramsey was her patient, and he'd wanted the chaplain to come so he could confess his sins. I guess the chaplain was tied up with another patient, so he ended up blurting everything out to her."

"What exactly did he say?" Kendra pressed.

He thought back to the strange conversation. "Per Helen, Stuart Ramsey admitted to sabotaging a plane six years ago. He said he'd caused the deaths of three people. Only he didn't know there would be three people aboard. When Helen asked if he had intended to kill them, he said he was paid to kill the pilot, not the others. And that he did it because he needed money. And that he wanted to confess so God would forgive him before he died."

"Wow. So basically my parents were collateral damage," Kendra murmured.

"Yeah." He swallowed a pang of guilt. It wasn't as if he had anything to do with Ramsey taking down the plane, but he still felt bad that she'd lost her parents because someone had wanted his father dead. "I'm sorry."

She shook her head. "Don't apologize. You're an innocent victim in this too."

He was touched by her comment. "If I had known some gunman would target me, I would have stayed in Billings."

She turned to look at him. "Makes me wonder how he knew your location, especially if you weren't followed."

As a computer nerd, he was keenly aware of how to track people electronically. Not that it was something he'd worried about until now. He dug his phone out of his pocket, then lowered his window and tossed it away.

Kendra gaped at him. "I'm not sure that was necessary."

"Yeah, I think that's the only way they could have known my location." He grimaced and held out his hand. "We'd better ditch yours, too, since I used mine to call you several times."

A pained expression crossed her features, but she pulled out her phone and handed it over. That one, too, went out the window.

"We'll need to get new phones," Kendra said, after a long moment of silence. "My family will go nuts if I don't let them know I'm okay."

"I understand." He couldn't imagine what it was like to have eight older siblings.

"What about you?" Kendra asked. "Don't you have a girlfriend or someone that you need to stay in touch with?"

"Nope." He thought about his former girlfriend, Shari Coffen. She'd broken things off a few months ago. Not that he'd missed her as much as he thought he would. "There's nobody special."

Her brow furrowed. "That's hard to believe."

He sighed. "My girlfriend dumped me for her personal trainer, who can bench-press twice his weight. Unlike me."

"She only cares about physical appearances?" Kendra waved a dismissive hand. "If that's the case, you're better off without her."

He smiled for what felt like the first time since crossing the Montana/Wyoming state line. "I can't disagree."

"Okay, when we get into Cody, we'll stop to buy disposable phones, then grab a bite to eat before finding a place to stay." She glanced at him. "Being a Monday, we shouldn't have too much trouble finding a hotel room."

"That sounds good." He relaxed a bit, relieved to have a plan. Yet he still wanted Kendra to head home after dropping him off at a hotel.

He had no idea why he was in danger, but at that

point, he needed to make sure Kendra didn't become collateral damage.

The way her parents had been.

As Kendra drove toward Cody, she kept a wary eye on the rearview mirror to make sure they weren't followed. When headlights came up behind her, she slowed down to the exact speed limit, moving over to encourage the driver to pass. So far, every vehicle had done exactly that.

Nobody followed the speed limit in Wyoming. Highway patrol didn't bother to pull anyone over unless they were going more than fifteen miles over the posted limit.

"I have my computer in my overnight bag," Dom said, breaking the silence. "I know how to reroute the ISP address to hide our location so we can dig into Stuart Ramsey without raising any red flags."

"You can do that?" She was impressed.

"Yeah. I'm all about the geeky stuff." He shifted in his seat, and she could tell by how his knees were wedged against the glove box that he wasn't comfortable.

"That's a good skill to have. I would love to learn how to do that."

He shrugged, avoiding her gaze. "I can teach you someday."

Someday? She frowned but then slowed her speed when she saw they were heading into Cody. Her stomach was growling, and she needed to feed Smoky too. There was a general store with disposable phones across from the Hitching Post Café. And that, in turn, was a block down from the Elk Lodge.

She turned into the store parking lot. "This is where we'll get new phones. We'll grab dinner across the street."

"Great." He pushed out of the car with enthusiasm. She opened the rear hatch for Smoky, then went around to grab her backpack so she'd have her K9's supplies. They could walk to the Post from here.

The task didn't take long, and less than ten minutes later, they were seated in a corner booth at the Hitching Post Café. Smoky crawled beneath the table to stretch out at Kendra's feet. She would feed the dog once they'd placed their orders. Thankfully, the Sullivan K9s were well known, and nobody demanded that Smoky stay outside.

A harried server brought menus and water glasses. "Can I get you something to drink?"

"Coffee for me," Dom said without looking up from the menu.

"I'll have the same." Kendra suspected he planned to stay up late digging into Stuart Ramsey's background to figure out why he'd sabotaged his father's plane. And if so, she intended to stick close. She wanted answers as to why her parents had died so tragically just as much as he did.

"Looks like they have a pot roast special." Dom grinned. "I love a good pot roast."

"Me too." It wasn't as good as their housekeeper Anna's, but it would hit the spot. She set her menu aside and rummaged in the backpack.

"Your dog is so well behaved." Dom leaned back to look under the table. "I barely know she's around."

"All of our K9s are well trained. But yes, Smoky isn't as vocal as some dogs." She drew out the collapsible dishes and set them on the floor beside her. Then she poured the water out of her glass into one of them.

"Are you ready to order?" Their server set two cups of coffee on the table.

"We'll both have the pot roast special." Kendra handed her the menus. "Thanks."

When the woman left, Kendra filled Smoky's bowl with food and set it on the floor beside the water dish. Smoky lifted her head and sniffed but didn't jump up to eat.

"Here, girl." She gestured to the dish. "Come and

get it." With permission, Smoky crawled out and ate with enthusiasm.

"Amazing," Dom murmured.

When the K9 was finished, Kendra tucked the dishes and food away. "The Elk Lodge has a suite." She sipped her coffee, eyeing Dom over the rim. "I think that's the best place for us to stay tonight."

"Us?" His eyes widened. "I told you to head home, Kendra. What if this gunman figures out where I'm staying?"

"All the more reason I need to stick with you." She glanced at Smoky beneath the table. "My K9 will alert us to danger. Besides, you don't have a vehicle."

He frowned. "I don't want you to be here."

She told herself there was no reason to be hurt by his comment. He wasn't trying to avoid her on a personal level.

At least, she didn't think so.

"I'm staying." She leveled him with a direct look. "I want to know what's going on, Dom. And if something happens to you, I'll never know why my parents had to die."

He sighed and scrubbed his hands over his face. "They didn't have to die. That's the point. Learning more about why my dad was targeted won't change that."

He was right, but she didn't care. She wasn't leaving. "We'll figure out what's going on, together."

"I never should have come here," he said, half under his breath.

"I'm glad you did." Again, she tried not to be upset by his comment. Sure, she'd secretly thought him to be good looking, but that wasn't why she'd reached out to him. Her goal had been to uncover the truth about that fateful night six years ago.

Their pot roast dinners arrived a few minutes later. Kendra hesitated, then said, "I'd like to say grace."

Dom froze in the act of picking up his fork. Then he dropped his hands into his lap. "Okay."

"Dear Lord Jesus, we ask You to bless this food we are about to eat. We also ask You to keep Dominic safe in Your care. Amen."

There was a long pause, before Dom echoed, "Amen."

She smiled, glad he'd participated, then dug into her meal. Dom did the same. They ate in silence for several minutes. The pot roast was better than she remembered.

Or maybe it was just that she was unusually hungry.

"Do you always pray before meals?" Dom arched a brow. "Or was that for my benefit?"

"Sullivans always pray before meals." She tipped

her head to the side, regarding him thoughtfully. "But if you want the truth, the prayer was mostly for your benefit. I am worried that gunman will try to find you. We need the Lord's protection as much as we need to understand what's going on, before the gunman strikes again."

He looked exasperated. "Like I said before, that's my problem. Not yours."

She shook her head. "We don't turn our backs on people in need. Besides, your life being is in danger is no joke." A sudden thought struck. "Do you think the nurse's phone call explaining about the confession is the reason why you've become a target?"

"I considered that, but I'm not sure why it would. Again, I don't know anything other than what she told me." He scowled. "We can reach out to Helen again. I have her contact information, including her email. She caught me at work but then used my personal email to communicate after that. However, she told me that Stuart Ramsey didn't identify the person who'd hired him. I guess the guy died before he had the chance."

"Yeah, but maybe the guy who did hire him isn't aware of that." She turned that possibility over in her mind. "Maybe he thinks Helen told you his name. Did Helen also report the confession to the police?"

"She did, yes." He sighed. "I think she called me first, though. Not sure why I was her priority, but she took the time to find me through my employer, Data Intelligence Services. I'm listed on their website as the manager, and I guess my contact information popped up when she searched on my name. She wanted me to know my father was murdered."

Murdered. Not an accident, but murder. For six years, Kendra had believed the crash was intentional, and now she knew for sure. Her parents hadn't been the target, but they'd been ruthlessly killed all the same.

"If Helen found you that easily, then there's no reason the man who hired Stuart Ramsey couldn't do the same." She frowned again. "So why now? Why come after you all these years later?"

"I don't know." His brow furrowed. "Has to be because of the confession, right?"

"We'll figure it out." She forced a reassuring smile on her face. "Your computer skills should make this a piece of cake."

He didn't look convinced, but he didn't argue either. When their server brought their bill, Dom grabbed it. "Dinner is on me. And I really think you need to head back to the ranch."

She was tired of repeating herself, so she ignored him. She wasn't leaving, no matter what. But she would have to call her brother Chase. She didn't want him to worry.

She slid out of the booth, then snagged her pack. Smoky crawled out from beneath the table, stretched, and then stood at her side, looking up expectantly.

"I know, you probably need to get busy, huh?" She bent to stroke Smoky's fluffy fur. "Soon."

Smoky's high curvy tail wagged back and forth in response.

Dominic left cash on the table, then followed her and Smoky outside. She paused near a snow-covered area and waved a hand. "Get busy."

Her K9 didn't need to be told twice. The Alaskan malamute trotted over to do her thing. Pulling a baggie out of her backpack, Kendra cleaned up after the dog, then tossed the waste in the trash.

"Good girl." She turned toward Dominic. "Are you ready? We left my SUV across the street."

"Yeah." He scowled. "I really wish you'd go home."

"Give it a rest, Dom. I'm a grown woman who can make my own decisions, thanks very much." Swallowing her annoyance, she gave Smoky the hand signal to come.

The dog trotted beside her as they crossed the café parking lot, then waited for a break in the traffic. She took a moment to appreciate how the main street of Cody was fully decorated for Christmas. Tiny twinkling blue lights shimmered along the rooftops of buildings and wreaths with large red bows hung from each streetlight. The holiday was still three weeks away, but Kendra knew that normally she'd only spend time in downtown Cody if she was shopping for Christmas gifts for her growing family.

Instead, she was digging into a six-year-old murder.

They crossed the street and approached her vehicle. They were only a few feet away when Smoky began to growl. Kendra paused, glancing around in concern. Smoky was even-tempered, she rarely growled at strangers.

"What is it, girl?" She kept her voice low. "What's gotten your attention?"

Dominic stopped beside her. "Is there a problem?"

"Maybe." She thought about some of the stories her older siblings had told, about how their K9s had focused on the bad guy's scent, alerting them to impending danger even without being asked to search.

Was that happening now? Was Smoky alerting her to the scent of the gunman?

"Kendra, get down!" Dominic reached over to

yank her behind the SUV just as the crack of gunfire
rang out. She snagged Smoky, drawing the dog close
as she silently prayed for God to keep them safe.

3

This was exactly what Dom had been afraid of! That bullet had come far too close to striking Kendra. And him. But his safety was secondary. He couldn't bear the thought of her getting hurt because some whack job had decided to kill him.

And he really didn't understand how this guy had found them again. Especially after they'd ditched their phones.

"Lord Jesus, keep us safe in Your care!" Kendra's whispered prayer only made him feel worse. She didn't deserve to be in danger like this.

Covering her with his body as much as possible, he lifted his head to find the location of the shooter. He narrowed his gaze on a large dark truck. The engine roared to life, twin headlights flashing on, blinding him. The vehicle backed up, then abruptly turned and drove away. Two seconds later, the wail of police sirens filled the air. At least this time, someone had heard the gunfire and called 911. Unlike when he'd been pinned down at the Redwood Motel.

"We need to get out of here." He straightened, tugging on Kendra's arm to draw her upright. "I think that black truck that just left belongs to the shooter."

"It looked like the one that barreled past me when I was driving toward the Redwood Motel." She stroked her hand over Smoky's fur. "We should stay to talk to the police."

He swallowed hard, knowing she was right. They'd left the Redwood Motel without sticking around, so they needed to follow through this time.

Maybe the local cops could give him a ride so Kendra and Smoky could head back to the ranch. He was convinced she'd change her mind about sticking close after this.

"Fine. We'll wait to give our statement." He gestured to the SUV. "Do you want to wait in the car where it's warmer?"

She shook her head. "There's no point, that's them pulling in now."

Red and blue flashing lights lit up the sky as the police cruiser slowed and turned into the parking lot of the store. Across the street, he noticed their server from the Hitching Post stood in the front doorway of the café, watching with interest. She must have been the one to call the police.

Wishing he understood what was going on, he waited for the police officer to emerge from the vehicle. Kendra stepped forward, her hand resting on Smoky's head.

"Hi, Burt." Her smile was strained. "Thanks for coming.

"Hey, Kendra. What's going on?" The burly officer turned toward him, his eyes narrowing with suspicion. "Who are you?"

Dom wasn't sure if Kendra being on a first-name basis with the local law enforcement was a good thing or a bad one. "Dominic Lakeland, here visiting from Billings, Montana."

Burt glanced back at Kendra. "He's a friend of yours?"

"Yes," she answered without hesitation. "Unfortunately, this is the second time he's been targeted by gunfire in a matter of hours. The first incident was at the Redwood Motel in Greybull. Now this."

Burt's brows hiked up. "Twice, huh? Any idea who might be responsible?"

"No clue." He hesitated, unsure of how much to tell him. "I recently learned the plane crash that killed my father and Kendra's parents was intentional. The only thing I can figure out is that these recent incidents are related to the past."

Burt stared at him for a long moment. "I'm not sure that's a logical assumption. Maybe you have other enemies that you're not telling us about?"

"I don't." He frowned. "I work for a computer firm. Nothing dangerous about what we do. I would never lie about something like that. If I knew who was responsible, I would tell you."

Burt shrugged, then looked at Kendra. "Do your siblings know about this?"

"Not yet." When the older cop scowled, she hastily added, "Don't worry, I plan to call them soon."

"Okay, tell me exactly what happened," Burt said.

"We ate dinner at the Hitching Post," Dom said. "We had stopped at the store earlier and left Kendra's SUV parked in the lot since the café is right across the street. We were on our way back when I caught a glimpse of a man lifting a handgun. He fired at us, then jumped into a dark truck and drove away."

"Dom saw more than I did," Kendra said. "I didn't see the man with a gun, I only heard the gunfire as Dom told me to get down."

"Did you notice the make or model of the dark truck?" Burt asked.

"It's a large pickup truck, maybe a GMC?" Dom wished he was better with cars. "I didn't get a good look at it. Things happened fast, and from this angle, I couldn't get the license plate."

"I saw a dark truck leaving the area of the Redwood Motel in Greybull as I approached," Kendra added. "I think that may have been the shooter."

"It's not much to go on," Burt muttered. "Can you ask Smoky to search for shell casings?"

"Of course. In fact, Smoky found one earlier." Kendra dug in her pocket and held up the brass. Burt pulled an evidence bag from his pocket so she could drop it inside. "That's from the parking lot of the Redwood Motel."

"Got it." Burt tucked it away as Kendra turned to her K9.

"Are you ready, girl?" She injected enthusiasm into her tone. "Are you? Search! Search for gold!"

Dom watched with interest as Smoky lowered her snout and sniffed along the parking lot. Less than a minute later, the dog stopped and pressed her nose into the snow. Then Smoky sat and let out a sharp bark.

Kendra and Burt hurried over. Kendra tugged the stuffed hippo from her backpack. "Good girl, Smoky! Good girl!" She tossed the hippo into the air. Smoky leaped up to grab it.

"I'm always amazed at how quickly they can find

brass." Burt pulled another evidence bag from his pocket and used it like a glove to pick up the shell casing. Dom had to admit, Kendra's K9 was impressive.

"Are they the same type of ammo?" Kendra asked.

"Looks like it, but we'll need to get both casings to the lab. Even then we'll have to match it with a weapon before we can say they were fired from the same gun." Burt shrugged. "It's better than nothing."

"If you need Logan to fly the brass to the state lab in Cheyenne, I'm sure he wouldn't mind." Kendra watched her dog for a moment, then held out her gloved hand. "Come, Smoky. Hand."

The fluffy dog trotted over and dropped the hippo into Kendra's palm.

"Good girl." She tucked the hippo away but then lavished the dog with attention. "You're such a good girl."

Smoky's curvy tail wagged back and forth like a rapid metronome. Under different circumstances, Dom would have smiled.

But he hated knowing Kendra and her K9 were in danger because of him.

"Burt, can you give me a lift to a different hotel?" Dom figured staying at the Elk Lodge so close to the site of the shooting was a bad idea. "That way Kendra can head back to the ranch."

"I'm not leaving." Her exasperated tone annoyed him. She narrowed her gaze. "Stop telling me what to do, Dom. We agreed to work together on this."

"That was before some creep started shooting at me." He turned to Burt. "Tell her she needs to get out of here."

"Kendra, you know Chase would want you to be safe." To his surprise, Burt voiced his agreement. "Better for you to head home and let the police handle this."

"Thanks, Burt. I'll make sure Chase knows you told me to go home." Kendra flashed Dom a look of reproach. "Let's get into the SUV. I'll take us to the Frontier. That's another hotel my family has used before."

The December wind kicked up, making her shiver. Since he wanted her to be warm, he reluctantly nodded. "Fine. Let's go."

"I'll be in touch," Burt said as Kendra opened the rear hatch for Smoky.

"I'll call you with my new phone number." Kendra closed the back hatch, then went to slide in behind the wheel. "We're using untraceable devices."

For all the good that had done, Dom thought sourly. Here he'd assumed they'd been tracked via his phone. Now he wasn't sure what more he could do to cover their tracks.

Burt nodded, then turned back to his cruiser. She started the engine and backed out of the parking spot. Soon they were heading down the road to the other side of Cody.

A strained silence fell between them. Obviously, she was annoyed with him. Why he was the bad guy for wanting her to be safe, he had no idea.

"I don't want you or Smoky to get hurt, Kendra," he said, finally breaking the silence. "Why is that so difficult for you to understand?"

"I don't want you to be hurt either." She glanced at him, then focused back on the road. "Seriously, Dom, don't you think we're safer together?"

"Not really." He shifted in his seat, trying to make more leg room. "You're safer on your own, without me."

"You don't know that." Kendra sighed. "Let's just say this shooter has come after you because he thinks you know his identity. Or the identity of the man who hired Stuart Ramsey. Maybe he believes the confession included more details about the crime. By now, he'll assume we've talked and that I know everything you do."

He hated to admit she had a point. "But we don't know anything."

"Yeah, see, I'm not sure that matters." She glanced at him. "The sooner we do know what's going on, the better. And that's why we need to work together on this."

Normally, Dom was known as a team player. He led his software team without difficulty.

But maybe she was right about this shooter assuming they knew more than they did. Otherwise, why come after him with literally guns blazing?

"Fine. We'll work together."

"Good." Kendra held his gaze. "We're going to figure this out."

He nodded without saying anything more. All he could do was hope that sticking with Kendra and Smoky wasn't a huge mistake.

Kendra took several turns through town, doubling back more than once to make sure they weren't followed. Clearly, her attempt to avoid being followed from Greybull hadn't been good enough. She'd thought that by encouraging cars behind her to pass would work. But she must have been followed anyway.

She wouldn't make that mistake again.

It irked her to think she'd inadvertently allowed this guy to find them. She was sure her older siblings would have done a better job, which only made her more determined to get to the bottom of this mess.

She'd repeatedly informed her family she wasn't a kid anymore. It was time to prove it. To them, but more so to herself. She and Dom would crack the case, making sure the man who'd hired Stuart Ramsey would be found and arrested.

The Great Frontier Hotel wasn't quite as nice as the Elk Lodge, but it would do. She pulled in and parked along the back of the property, making sure her SUV couldn't be seen from the road.

Wordlessly, they emerged from the SUV. A quick glance around proved there were no dark trucks in sight.

"Come, Smoky." Kendra pulled her backpack from the SUV, looping it over her shoulder. Good thing she had a change of clothes. Smoky went to get busy, before coming over to stand beside her. Dominic pulled his overnight case from the back seat and joined her.

Together, they headed inside. The sudden bright lights of the lobby made her squint. Dom towered over her, and his long stride had him reaching the counter first. "Do you have a suite available?"

"Yes." The clerk smiled. "What's your name?"

"Sullivan," Kendra said quickly. "Put the reservation under Sullivan."

"Of course." The clerk tapped the name into her computer.

Dom frowned but didn't argue. She knew it wasn't much of a disguise, but she hoped that leaving Dominic's name off the reservation might help. His scowl deepened when she handed the clerk her credit card.

"I'm not here to mooch off you," he said in a low voice. "I would rather pay my own way."

"I know that. You bought dinner after all. This is an attempt to keep you safe." She took the keys and led the way down the hall to their first-floor suite. "Besides, I'm the one who insisted on sticking close."

He didn't respond, simply standing aside as she unlocked the door. She hoped he wasn't going to be cranky all evening.

The suite had two bedrooms. She headed to the one to the right, leaving him to claim the other. Smoky followed her inside, sniffing the perimeter with interest. Kendra set her backpack down, then removed the collapsible water bowl and the .38.

"You have a gun?" Dom gaped in surprise.

"It was in my backpack." She felt a little foolish for not mentioning it sooner, especially under the circumstances. "Chase trained me to hit what I'm aiming for. But obviously, having it tucked away wasn't the smartest move on my part. I have a belt holster I can use from this point forward."

"My dad taught me to shoot when I was a kid." Dom grimaced. "Now that I know he was murdered, I'm looking at everything we did back then in a different light. Makes me wonder if he suspected he might be in danger someday."

She nodded thoughtfully, filling the bowl with water and setting it down for Smoky. "Was your dad always a charter pilot?"

"For as far back as I can remember." Dom pulled a laptop from his overnight case and set it on the table. "My mom died when I was three. I don't remember her at all."

"That must have been hard." Kendra knew she and her siblings were blessed to have had their parents' love and support. They had been married for thirty-eight years when they died.

"It was harder for my dad," Dom said. "He never remarried. To be honest, I can't even imagine why anyone would have paid Stuart Ramsey to sabotage his plane." Dom dropped into a chair and began working on the computer.

"How are you going to hide your ISP?" She leaned over his shoulder to watch. "I've heard of that capability but have no idea how it works."

Over the next few minutes, Dom described how he planned to reroute his ISP to hide their identity and their location. She found the information interesting, but also far more technically advanced than she'd anticipated. Kendra doubted she'd remember how to do this again if needed.

While she'd taken over most of the computer work for her family's ranch, updating social media and renting cars and homes for her siblings as needed, her skills were nowhere near as good as Dominic's.

She activated the new phones and powered them up, knowing she couldn't put off calling Chase much longer. She wouldn't put it past Burt Jones to call him first.

"Is this Kendra?" Her oldest brother's voice held a mixture of concern and anger.

"Yes, Chase. I'm fine, nothing for you to worry about."

"Where are you?" Anger overwhelmed the hint of concern. "I can't believe you took off without telling anyone where you were going!"

She looked up at the ceiling, striving for patience. "Are you going to listen to what I have to say? Or continue to lecture me?"

She imagined steam blasting out of his ears, but to his credit, Chase didn't explode. "Kendra, what is going on?"

"I'm with Dominic Lakeland. He's the son of the pilot who was killed alongside our parents. We have new information that proves the crash wasn't an accident. A man by the name of Stuart Ramsey was paid to sabotage the plane."

Chase didn't say anything for a long moment. "Why would anyone want our parents dead?"

"Dominic's father, Gary Lakeland, was the real target. According to the man who confessed, he didn't know our parents would be on the plane. That was part of the guilt that was eating at him all these years."

Another long silence. "Where are you staying?"

Kendra knew her brother would hop into his vehicle and drive out there the moment she revealed their location. "Wyn is pregnant, and you have Eli to consider. I don't need your help at this point. We're safe. We're only using disposable phones as a precautionary measure." That wasn't the full truth, and she squelched the stab of guilt. "Please, Chase, I'm asking you to trust my judgment. If we run into trouble, I'll call you, or one of the other siblings. I promise I won't be reckless."

"Taking off without a word to anyone in the family was reckless," he shot back. "I don't appreciate being kept in the dark about this new information. We all care about what happened six years ago."

She knew that was true, but she was the only one who'd insisted the crash was no accident. She was the one who'd requested the police broaden their investigation. Something that hadn't happened, mostly because they hadn't been able to find enough of the plane to determine what had happened one way or the other.

It was only because of Ramsey's confession that they knew now the plane engine had been tampered with. Discovering how it had been brought down wasn't as important as understanding why.

Especially now that Dom was in danger.

"I don't like this, Kendra. You're usually more level-headed than this."

She rolled her eyes, knowing he couldn't see her response. This was Chase's attempt to convince her to act more responsibly. Even though he had run headfirst into danger back when his son, Eli, had been kidnapped. "I called so you and the others wouldn't worry. That's being responsible. I'll let you know if I need anything more. That's also being responsible. For now, we're going to keep digging into Stuart Ramsey's background to see what we can uncover."

Another long silence. Then, "You're being awfully stubborn."

"Why are you surprised? Stubbornness is a big part of the Sullivan DNA. I'll be in touch, Chase." With that, she ended the call. Setting the phone aside, she fully expected Chase to call her right back.

But he didn't.

"Your brother sounds concerned about you." Dom glanced at her, then turned his attention back to the computer screen. "He'll blame me if anything happens to you."

"No, he won't hold my decision against you." She couldn't deny feeling relieved that the dreaded call home was behind her. "Are you sure your dad didn't have another career? One prior to being a charter pilot?"

"I don't appreciate you insinuating my dad had done something so bad that he was murdered."

"I didn't say he did anything bad, but maybe he was a witness to a crime. Something that caused someone to silence him, permanently."

She half expected him to snap in outrage, but he turned and stared at her for a long moment. Then he nodded slowly. "I think that's it."

"What? That your dad witnessed a crime?"

"Yeah." Dom scrubbed his hands over his face. "I think my dad was originally from the East Coast."

She pulled up a chair to sit beside him. "What makes you say that?"

"Back when I was twelve or so, a family moved to Montana from New Jersey. I invited my new friend Toby to my house after school. I told my dad he had a funny accent. My dad told me not to tease him, that it's not his fault he grew up in another state. But within an hour of Toby being there, my dad started talking with an East Coast accent. I thought he was teasing Toby, but when I mentioned it, he turned pale and immediately stopped talking." He shook his head. "It never occurred to me that he may have once lived in New Jersey. When I had to do a family tree for school, he told me we always lived in Montana. That my grandparents on both sides of the family were dead and that we had no cousins, aunts, or uncles." Dom let out a harsh laugh. "Even my teacher thought it was strange we didn't have any extended family."

She stared at him. "You think your dad was placed in witness protection?"

He spread his hands. "I honestly don't know. But it makes sense, don't you think?" Dom turned and pulled up the website for the US Marshals Service. "Maybe I need to call them to find out."

"It's too late to do that tonight." For some reason, she didn't like the idea of making the call. Granted, their phones couldn't be easily traced, but giving away their location seemed counterintuitive. "My sister-in-law Raine used to work for the marshals. We can reach out to her if you'd like."

"If she's not a marshal now, I'm not sure that will help. I'll leave a message." Dom picked up the phone and dialed the number. She could hear a canned voice mail response on the other end of the line. "This is Dominic Lakeland, my father was Gary Lakeland, he died in a plane crash six years ago. A gunman has taken several shots at me in the past few hours. I need to know if I'm in trouble because of whatever my father might have witnessed at some point. Please call me back at this number. Thanks." He lowered the phone. "That should get someone's attention. I bet we hear back from them first thing in the morning."

"Yeah." She forced a smile. "It would be nice to get some answers."

Dom stared up at the ceiling for a long moment. "I wonder why my dad never mentioned being a witness to a crime. I was twenty-two when he died. I can see keeping a secret when I was a kid, but once I was an adult, he should have come clean."

"Honestly, Dom, let's not jump to conclusions." She reached over to touch his arm. "We don't know for sure he was in witness protection. Maybe this is more related to a charter he did at one point or another. My brother-in-law Logan ended up transporting drugs in his plane, something he never would have done willingly. My sister Jess helped him uncover the truth, but they were both in danger because of a crime that he'd unwittingly participated in."

Dom frowned. "I hadn't thought of that. My dad could have chartered a criminal who thought my dad knew more than he should."

"Exactly." She managed a reassuring smile. "Let's keep digging into Stuart Ramsey's background. He's the one who committed the crime."

"That makes sense." Dom's expression turned sheepish. "Sorry to go off the deep end."

"Don't worry about it. The worst that can happen is that someone from the US Marshals office calls back to say you're crazy." She offered a teasing smile.

Dom turned back to the computer and began a deep dive into Stuart Ramsey. "I'm surprised Helen gave me his date of birth."

"Confidentiality rules don't matter once a person is dead." Her brother Trevor, who was an EMT, had often explained that he couldn't talk about patients because of confidentiality. In this case, she'd give Helen the benefit of the doubt.

Dom nodded, but his attention was on the screen. After a few minutes, he turned to look at her. "Guess who worked in Jackson Hole as a plane mechanic?"

"Stuart? Really?" She leaned in to see the screen. "I wonder why he wasn't questioned about the crash."

"Stuart Ramsey didn't live or work in Montana,

so he wouldn't have been on anyone's radar." Dom frowned. "Not sure how the man who paid him stumbled across him."

"Lots of wealthy people vacation in Jackson, maybe the guy who paid him chartered a plane and met him at the hangar." She was about to say more when Smoky abruptly lifted her head and pricked her ears forward. The K9 stared at the door, then slowly stood and began to growl low in her throat.

A sliver of unease snaked down Kendra's spine. "What is it, girl?"

"Get down." Dom grabbed her .38 as she bent to drag Smoky beneath the table seconds before a barrage of bullets slammed into the hotel room door.

4

It had been years since Dom fired a gun, but he didn't hesitate to return fire at whoever was on the other side of the hotel room door. He fired several rounds, which must have caught the shooter by surprise because the gunfire abruptly stopped. Dom glanced at Kendra, and whispered, "Get into the bedroom."

"You too. We're getting out of here." She grabbed the computer off the table, snagged the backpack with her other hand, and bolted across the room. As the shooting had stopped, Dom figured she was right about getting out of there. He followed Smoky into the bedroom where Kendra was wrenching the window open.

He gave her credit for thinking on her feet. She straddled the window frame and ducked through.

When she was standing on the ground outside, she looked at her K9. "Come."

The dog gracefully leaped through the opening. Dominic could see Kendra's SUV; she'd parked in the back of the lot, which happened to be closer to the windows of their suite than the front lobby. Then he threw his leg over the windowsill. The opening was small, making it difficult for him to get through, but he managed. By the time he was outside, Kendra was halfway to the SUV, using the key fob to open the back hatch.

Without needing to be told, Smoky jumped into the crate area. Kendra tossed the backpack in beside her K9. Dominic hurried to the passenger side of the car as Kendra slid in behind the wheel, dropping the laptop on the floor at Dom's feet. Seconds later, they were driving out of the parking lot.

There was no sign of the large black truck, though. Dom frowned, wondering where the shooter had left it. Two police cars were heading toward the hotel, red and blue lights flashing.

"Do you think you hit the shooter?" Kendra asked once they were headed in the opposite direction from the police. "He stopped when you returned fire."

"Maybe." Dom tried not to think about the possibility he'd killed someone. He'd only fired in self-defense, without taking the time to think it through.

Now he dropped the gun in the center console as if distancing himself from the weapon would make him feel better. He swiveled in his seat, glancing around to make sure there was no black truck following them. Satisfied, he settled back. "My goal was to force him to back off."

"I'm glad you jumped into action." Kendra held his gaze for a moment. "If not for your quick response, we wouldn't have had time to escape."

He nodded, knowing she was right. Logically, he knew it wasn't his fault someone was trying to kill him. Not that he wanted to be responsible for someone's death no matter the circumstances. "I don't think it's a coincidence that I left that message for the US Marshals Service and an hour later the gunman showed up at our hotel."

Kendra frowned. "I think we need to reach out to Justin's wife, Raine. She can help us figure out who to trust."

The last thing he wanted to do was drag more innocent people into this nightmare. Yet what other choice did they have? It seemed that this gunman was able to track him down no matter where they went. If he didn't know better, he'd think he had a tracking device implanted on his body.

Worst of all, he hated how Kendra and Smoky were in danger too.

"You can call Raine for her input." He sighed,

then added, "Maybe she can head out to pick you up. This latest incident proves you need to return to the ranch."

"Stop trying to get rid of me." Kendra's tone was sharp with irritation. "I'm not leaving you alone."

"Kendra, your concern for me is admirable, but what if one of those bullets had killed you?" He turned to stare at her. "Do you have any idea how terrible I'll feel if you die because of me?"

"Same goes." She glanced at him, then turned her attention back to the road. "I would feel awful if you died because I left for the safety of the ranch. Besides, it's a good thing I was with you since you ended up using my gun to return fire."

Dom sighed, then decided to give up. Kendra was the most stubborn woman he'd ever known. Yet she had a point about the weapon. At least they weren't entirely helpless.

He looked around again, relieved that Kendra had gotten away from the hotel without drawing attention. They'd need to talk to the police at some point too.

"Do you have a destination in mind?" he asked, changing the subject. She seemed to be driving randomly through town, making several turns. "I don't think we should head to another hotel."

"I agree another hotel wouldn't be smart." She frowned as she made yet another turn. He understood she was trying to avoid being followed. "There's a cabin northwest of Cody that I rented for my brothers a few months ago. We need to see if that's available."

"Is that why you grabbed the computer? So you can find a rental property?"

"Yeah, and we still need to dig into Stuart Ramsey's background." She wrinkled her nose. "The problem is that I don't want to pull over to use the computer now. I figure I'll simply drive to the cabin, see if anyone happens to be there."

"What if there are people staying there?" He wasn't sure just showing up was a good idea. "Then we're back to square one. We can't just drive around all night."

"It's possible." She shrugged. "I figure it can't hurt to check it out. If it's not open, we can pull over and try to find another place to stay."

He shifted, trying to get his legs into a more comfortable position, then reached for the laptop she'd tossed on the floor. "I'll see if I can find something."

They rode in silence for several minutes. He'd barely started his search when his disposable phone rang, startling him. He pulled it from his pocket and eyed the number. Was this the US Marshals Service returning his call? He didn't think anyone else had this number. Kendra had used her phone to call her family. He hadn't contacted anyone other than the marshals.

He debated ignoring it but then realized that answering while on the move was probably better than waiting until they were settled in someplace. "Yeah?"

"Is this Dominic Lakeland?" the male voice on the other end of the line asked.

"Yep." Feeling Kendra's curious gaze, he made a circle with his index finger, indicating she should keep driving around. "Who are you?"

"This is US Marshal Andrew Levy. Your call was routed to me since the marshal who originally relocated your father twenty-four years ago has retired."

Hearing the news was like a sucker punch to the gut. His father really had been relocated to Montana in the witness protection program. Even though that had been his theory, it was a whole different thing to hear it spoken by someone in charge.

"Dominic? Are you still there?" Levy asked.

"Yes." He glanced at Kendra. "I'm here. I need some answers about why someone keeps trying to kill me."

"Where are you now?" Levy demanded.

"You don't need to know my current location." He wasn't convinced this guy was legit. What if he was somehow connected to the shooter? The timing of the gunman showing up at the hotel was too close to the call he'd made for his peace of mind. "Why don't you tell me what's going on?"

"I'd be happy to fill you in, but it's better if we meet in person." Levy's tone sounded calm and rational. Dom felt the exact opposite. He was suspicious and on edge.

"No." He took a slow deep breath to calm his racing heart. "I'm not going anywhere until I know more. You can either fill me in, or I'll figure out the truth some other way."

He held his breath, waiting for Levy's response. "Okay, I understand you have concerns. I would prefer not to have this conversation over the phone, but suffice it to say, I thought the danger was over once your father's plane went down."

Dom almost mentioned Stuart Ramsey's confession but caught himself in time. Levy should be the one giving him information, not the other way around. "Is that why you didn't bother to tell me about my dad being in the program?"

"Yes," Levy admitted bluntly. "We knew your father kept you in the dark; you were only three years old when he was relocated. Once he was gone, there was no reason to dredge up the past."

Dom didn't agree with that sentiment. But all he said was "Go on."

"Your father was placed in the program because he provided key information against an organized crime syndicate. He testified against a man named Gunther Volter who is still serving a life sentence in federal prison."

The news was shocking, but he did his best to remain calm. "Did you have reason to believe Gunther Volter paid someone to make sure my dad's plane crashed?"

"No, we didn't suspect that at all. Your father's mayday call didn't indicate foul play. We thought the crash was weather related." Levy paused, then said, "But that was before we learned the plane had been sabotaged. When the local law enforcement received a call from the nurse who'd taken Stuart Ramsey's confession, we realized the crash was no accident."

Dom glanced at Kendra, knowing she was listening to his side of the conversation with interest. "Okay, why would Gunther Volter come after me now?"

"I can't think of a single reason," Levy admitted. "Which is why I think we need to meet in person. There must be something we're missing."

Dom wasn't willing to do that, at least not yet. Inside, he was still reeling from discovering his father testified against a crime syndicate. "Is this the number I should use to reach you? I need to think about this before I commit to a meeting."

A long silence stretched between them. Finally,

Levy sighed loudly. "Yes. This is my cell number. You can call me anytime. But, Dominic, don't wait too long. If the cartel is involved and thinks you know something that could hurt them, you're in grave danger."

With the recent shooting all too fresh in his mind, he considered that to be a gross understatement. Yet he didn't mention the details of what had gone down at the hotel, primarily because he didn't want Levy to know he was in Wyoming. Also, he remained suspicious of the timing of the attack. "I'll be in touch." He ended the call and grimaced. "I'm sure you heard my side of the conversation. That was US Marshal Andrew Levy returning my call."

"I guess you were right about your father being in witness protection." She glanced at him, then asked, "Are you okay?"

He was far from okay, but there was no point in dwelling on the realization his father had been a criminal. Or at least involved enough in the criminal organization that he'd testified against Gunther Volter. "Yeah. Except for the fact that I don't trust this Levy guy as far as I can throw him."

"I think it's time to call my sister-in-law Raine. I'm sure she can verify Levy is legit." She grimaced, then added, "Not that he still couldn't be dirty."

"I don't like any of this." He stared blindly at the passing scenery. They were outside of the city now, with nothing but wilderness surrounding them. "It sounds like Gunther Volter, the man my father testified against, is still in prison. I guess this could be about revenge. Like he's angry that I'm living my life while he's in jail."

"Maybe. But if so, why wait until now? You've been living your life for six years since your dad passed away. And I still want to know why Gunther had your father murdered. Just for revenge? Or was there more to the story?"

"Those are good questions." He fell silent, still absorbing the news.

Kendra turned onto a driveway that hadn't been plowed since the last snowfall. The SUV bumped along the uneven surface until she brought it to a stop outside a large cabin. There were no lights on inside, and the lack of tire tracks indicated nobody had been there recently. "Well, it's vacant."

He nodded, eyeing the accommodations. The place looked nice enough. "How are you planning on getting in?"

"Sit tight, I'll see if the code works." She kept the engine idling as she pushed out of the driver's seat. She trudged through snow that reached the middle of her calves, then pushed buttons on the key lock.

With a triumphant expression, she held up a key ring. Five seconds later, she had the front door open.

Flipping on a light switch, she gestured for him to come inside.

He nodded and pushed his door open. Then he went around the back to open the back hatch for Smoky.

It was good to have a place to stay, especially one that was completely off-grid. Nobody knew they were there since they hadn't gone through a rental agency to secure the property.

If this mountain cabin in the middle of nowhere doesn't work to keep them safe, he thought darkly, *nothing will.*

KENDRA WAS RELIEVED the key code hadn't been changed since she'd last rented the place and made a mental note to make sure she reimbursed the owners once the danger was over. In the meantime, she hoped nobody else showed up in the next day or so.

Smoky bounded toward her, clearly thrilled to be out of the car and in the snow. "Get busy, girl," she said firmly.

Her K9 whirled and leaped through the snow to do her thing. Kendra wanted to believe they were safe there, but she intended to turn the SUV around so that they could drive straight down to the road if needed.

Dom brought the computer inside, setting it on the kitchen counter. Unfortunately, they'd been forced to leave his overnight case behind at the hotel. She'd snagged the backpack and computer, her concern mostly to make sure she had food and protective gear for Smoky.

"I can't believe they didn't change the code." Dom glanced around the interior of the upscale cabin. "Especially since this is such a nice place."

"It's a little pricey, not the sort of place your average elk hunter would use." She glanced at the fireplace, shivering in the cold. She headed over to build a fire.

"Here, I can do that." Dom nudged her aside. "You mentioned calling your sister-in-law. I'd like to know what she can dig up about Marshal Andrew Levy."

"Okay." Kendra moved back toward the kitchen. Smoky followed, staying close to her side. Their K9s were well trained not to be skittish around gunfire, but she believed her dog sensed they were in danger.

"Good girl," she murmured, stroking her hand over Smoky's fluffy coat. "Lie down." Once her partner stretched out on the floor beside her, she pulled out her phone and punched in Raine's number.

Her sister-in-law answered on the second ring. "Hello?" Her wary tone was because of the unknown number.

"Raine, it's Kendra, obviously using a disposable phone." She figured Chase had already filled in the rest of her siblings on what was going on. "I need to ask about a US Marshal by the name of Andrew Levy. Do you know him? Or is there a way you can find some information out about him?"

"His name doesn't sound familiar," Raine said, "but I'm happy to ask around. What role does Levy play in your parents' plane crash?"

Kendra took a moment to explain about how Dominic had remembered his father using a New Jersey accent, along with the message he'd left for the marshals service. "An hour after Dom left the message, a gunman showed up at the hotel. We got away; everyone is fine," she said quickly. "But now Levy wants to meet with Dominic. He claims Dom's father testified against a man named Gunther Volter who is still serving a life sentence in federal prison."

"Wow, that's interesting." Raine was silent for a moment. "As you know, my old boss was dirty, and he's now dead. I reported to my new boss for barely a month before I resigned. I'm happy to call and ask him about Levy, but I'm not sure how much he'll tell me."

"We really need to know if we can trust Levy. Especially since the danger is ramping up big time. Not that Chase needs to hear that," she hastily added. "He'll just worry. But we're operating under the assumption that Gunther Volter must have hired someone to go after Dominic."

"Why do that after all this time has passed?" Raine asked. "Mob guys can be vicious about revenge, but Dominic didn't do anything. He was a kid. It's hard to imagine why they turned on him now."

"Exactly my point." The more she thought about it, the less Kendra understood the connection between whatever Dominic's father had testified to twenty-four years ago and the attempts against Dom now. "I guess we should cooperate with Levy, if he can be trusted."

"I'll make a few calls," Raine said. "Despite what happened with my boss a few months ago, it's rare to have US Marshals who can't be trusted."

"Thanks, Raine." It was nice to have someone to lean on. "If you could call me back at this number, that would be great."

"Will do. Are you sure you're safe?" Raine sounded concerned. "I can head out to stay with you and Dominic."

"We're safe. Nobody knows where we are," Kendra assured her. "But having additional information would be really helpful moving forward."

"I'll get back to you as soon as possible." With that, Raine ended the call.

"It must be nice to have family around to support you." Dom sighed. "For all I know, I have family back east who think I'm dead."

"This must be difficult for you." She couldn't imagine what it would be like learning her parents were in witness protection and killed out of some misguided revenge. "The good news is that your dad made the right decision to protect you."

"Yeah. I guess." Dom didn't look convinced. "I keep thinking back to my childhood. I can't help but wonder if everything my father told me was a lie."

"Don't think of it that way." Her heart ached for him. "I'm sure he wouldn't have lied if he had another option."

"Maybe he shouldn't have gotten involved with the cartel in the first place." Dom's voice was bitter.

She couldn't think of a way to make him feel better. "Your father probably didn't intend to get involved in the cartel. He may not have had a choice."

"There's always a choice." Dom abruptly turned and walked toward the fire. He stood with his back to her, clearly struggling with his emotions.

Rising to her feet, she crossed over to join him.

The warmth of the fire felt wonderful, taking the chill from the room. She put a hand on his arm. "Dominic, your father walked away from everyone he knew to provide a new life for you. Relocating from New Jersey to Montana of all places. Maybe he could have made better choices, but at the end of the day, he chose to protect you."

Dom reached over to cover her hand with his, as if grateful for the connection. "Are you always this positive? Determined to look on the bright side all the time?"

She couldn't help but smile. "Pretty much."

He nodded, grinning wryly. "I glad you're here with me, Kendra. It would be much worse learning about my father's past while being completely alone."

"We're going to get through this." She knew she was sounding all Pollyanna again.

His grin faded. "I'm trying to imagine how my dad got involved with a cartel in the first place. It sounds like something out of a movie."

"Hopefully, Raine will be able to shed some light on that." She briefly leaned her temple against his shoulder before reluctantly pulling away. "I should check out the food situation. We may not have much to eat for breakfast."

"Okay." He turned from the fire, following her

into the kitchen. "We can always head to the store for a few things."

She shrugged, thinking it would be best if they didn't go anywhere until they knew more about Andrew Levy. She opened the fridge. It was empty except for a couple of water bottles. With a sigh, she moved on to the cupboards. There were some cans of soup and two large cans of beef stew. They were better than nothing.

When her phone rang, she and Dom jumped and stared at the device as if it were a snake that might bite them. Recognizing Raine's number, she quickly answered. "Hey, Raine. Did you find something out for us?"

"I did. But you may want to put me on speaker so Dominic can hear this too."

"Hold on." She lowered the phone, put the call on speaker, then set the device in the center of the table. "Raine, Dominic is here. Dom, this is my sister-in-law Raine."

"Nice to meet you, Dom," Raine said. "Sorry it has to be during a time of trouble."

"Nice to meet you too. I'm sorry to have to ask for such a big favor," Dom admitted. "I'm still trying to assimilate what I've learned so far."

"Thankfully, my boss wants me to come back, so he filled me in on your father's case file. Normally, he wouldn't have access, but after your father's death, it wasn't considered to be as confidential."

"Okay." Dom's gaze seemed to cling to hers. Kendra reached over to take his hand. "What can you tell me?"

"Levy was right in that your father provided key information and testified against Gunther Volter," Raine said. "Your father was an accountant. He kept the books for an organization called Randover Royals. They were well known to be involved in illegal mining, primarily diamonds and gold. And there were allegations of other criminal activities as well, specifically expanding into drugs."

Dom swallowed hard. "My father knew they were criminals?"

"No, according to the file, he discovered they were running money through the company. He wanted to get out, but it was too late. He already knew too much." Raine paused for a moment. "What do you know about your mother's death?"

Dom's fingers tightened around hers. "According to my dad, my mother died in a car crash when I was three years old. Is that the truth? Or another lie?"

"That is the truth," Raine assured him. "But there's more. Your mother's crash was no accident. You were supposed to be in the car with her, but you had a fever, so your mom left you at home with a babysitter. The cartel assumed that once you and your mother were eliminated from the picture, your dad would keep quiet. Thankfully, you survived, and your father went straight to the authorities. He testified against Gunther Volter, and well, you know the rest."

Dom looked shell-shocked at the news. Kendra couldn't contain her surprise either. Bad enough that Dom's father had been murdered, but to learn his mother had been killed, too, was worse. The young mother and Dom were innocent victims.

And if they weren't careful, Dominic would end up dead too.

5

———

Murdered. Dom's mother and father had both been murdered! The truth was a heavy burden to bear, especially since his father's actions had ultimately killed Kendra's parents. With the recent gunfire still fresh in his mind, he forced himself to focus his scattered thoughts. The current danger had to be their priority. "Raine, do you think we can trust Levy?"

"I don't know." He admired her honesty. "I don't have a reason to distrust him, but based on the shooting at the hotel, you and Kendra should proceed with caution."

That sounded like a good plan to him. As far as Dom was concerned, he'd wait to call Levy the following morning. Maybe they could meet at a café for breakfast. Choosing neutral territory would be the best way to keep their current location safe.

Kendra nodded at him, as if reading his mind. "Raine, what do you know about the Randover Royals? I assume someone else is running the organization now that Gunther is in prison."

"Funny you should ask, because the organization allegedly disbanded after Gunther Volter's arrest." Raine's tone was dry. "In my opinion, those who weren't caught laid low just long enough to recreate themselves into something new and equally dangerous."

Dom sighed. "I still don't understand why anyone from the Randover Royals organization would come after me all these years later."

"A man by the name of Theo Le Ruiz was believed to be the real leader of the Randover Royals," Raine said. "From what I understand, Volter was the face of the company, but Le Ruiz pulled strings from South Africa."

"Wait a minute, South Africa?" When Levy had mentioned a drug cartel, Dom had assumed they were Mexican. Not from South Africa.

"Yeah, believe it or not, cartels are even more active in South Africa." Raine sighed. "Like I said, the cartels have their fingers in the gold and gemstone mining operations, along with adding drugs to the mix."

Gold and gemstones? Dominic fished in his pocket for his keys. Back when he'd gotten his driver's license, he'd found a strange coin on the floor of his father's plane hangar. His dad had told him it wasn't even worth a dollar, but rather than toss it out, he'd made the coin into a keychain. Staring down at the surface of the currency now, he saw the words South Africa along the side. "I have an old coin from South Africa. I found it years ago. My dad mentioned it wasn't worth much. I haven't really thought about it since."

"That's very interesting. Can you send me a picture of it?" Raine asked.

"Yeah." He glanced at Kendra as he used his phone to take a picture of the coin. Then he asked, "What's your phone number?"

Kendra rattled off the digits. He entered them into his new phone and sent the image.

"I have it." Raine sounded distracted. "Dom, do you know if your dad has more of these coins?"

"I doubt it. I've never seen any, and I cleaned out his stuff about a year after his death." Dom hadn't wanted to go through his father's personal items, but in the end, he'd wanted to at least donate his clothing and other items to those in need. "I would have found them."

"You're sure about that?" Raine pressed.

"Why are you asking?" Kendra frowned. "Is that a rare coin or something?"

"Or something," Raine agreed. "I'm not the expert on South African cartels, but this appears to be a Krugerrand coin."

He stared at Kendra, his thoughts whirling. "I don't know what that means."

"They're currency that was circulated in South Africa for years, then were banned," Raine explained. "I'm not sure why, but they don't make them anymore. And those that are floating around out in the world are now considered extremely valuable."

"How valuable?" Kendra asked.

"This coin alone could be worth up to four thousand dollars."

What? Four grand? For one stinking coin? Dom stared at his key ring. "Why would my father tell me this was worthless?"

"I don't have a good answer for that," Raine said with a sigh. "I'm trying to understand why he'd only have one coin."

He was still struggling to comprehend how one coin could be worth so much money. "Do you think he had others? Like a stash he'd taken when he'd relocated to Montana?"

"If you haven't found any, then I'd think this is the only one he had." Raine paused, then added,

"Unless he had some with him when the plane went down."

Dom had to admit that was a possibility. And if that was the case, those Krugerrand coins were likely gone for good. "The wreckage of the plane was never found."

"Except for the tail piece my sister Jess discovered," Kendra interjected. "We've searched the area around there but never found anything else. Granted, we didn't have a lot of time to spend looking for more, between doing all of our SAR missions."

Dom glanced out the window at the snow-blanketed ground. There was no way to mount a search now. Maybe in the spring? But that was months away, and besides, finding more coins wasn't nearly as important as finding and arresting the gunman who kept popping up to shoot at them.

"I know it's been busy," Raine said. "Just something to think about in the future."

"Yeah, but the Krugerrand can't be the reason I've been targeted by gunfire." Dom scowled. "Nobody knows I have this."

"True," Raine agreed. "I'm wondering, though, if the reason your father was killed was because Volter thought he'd stolen Krugerrand from him."

"Anything is possible," Kendra said. "I'd like to know how Gunther's people found Gary in Billings.

And if he wanted the coins back, why hire Stuart Ramsey to kill Dom's father? Especially taking down his plane. If the guy did have more coins, he'd likely keep them close at hand."

"Those are all good questions, and I wish I had answers for you." Raine sounded apologetic. "You may need to meet with Andrew Levy to learn more."

Meeting with Marshal Levy went against the grain, but Dom wasn't sure there was a way to avoid it. "I'm irked that Levy didn't mention the cartel was in South Africa."

"He may have kept information back to encourage a meeting," Raine pointed out. "Although I would have thought he'd understand that honesty would offer a better advantage than deceit."

"Raine, can you help by continuing to dig into Gunther Volter, Theo Le Ruiz, and the Randover Royals?" Kendra asked. "We can do that, too, but you might have more luck with accessing information known by the marshals."

"I'll do my best," Raine promised. "But you guys need to be careful. If the gunman tracking you is from the Randover Royal cartel, they're extremely dangerous."

"Thanks, Raine." Dom still wasn't sure why these guys were coming after him. Unless Stuart Ramsey's confession had spurred things along. Maybe Kendra was right in that Gunther Volter's people assumed Ramsey had said more than he should have.

"Yes, thanks," Kendra added. "We'll be in touch again soon."

"Kendra . . ." Raine sighed loudly. Then she added, "Please call for backup if things go bad. You shouldn't be handling this on your own."

"We're safe here," Kendra said firmly. "I promise there is no way we can be electronically tracked to this location."

"Okay, then. I'll call you later if I learn anything more." Raine sounded resigned as she disconnected from the call.

"May I see the Krugerrand?" Kendra asked. She leaned forward, close enough that he caught the flowery scent of her skin.

"Sure." He handed it over. "I feel a little silly knowing I made it into a key ring when it's worth so much."

A smile tugged at the corner of her mouth. When Smoky shifted and sighed at their feet, he gave in to the urge to stroke the dog's fluffy fur. "At least you didn't bore a hole through it. It looks like it's glued to something."

"I glued it over an old key ring I found." He shook his head, wondering again why his father had told him it was worthless. "It never occurred to me it might be made of real gold."

"Not just gold, but into a currency that is no longer made." Kendra took the key ring from his fingers, examining it closely. "I must admit, it doesn't look like anything special. Certainly nothing that's worth several thousand dollars."

"Yeah." He thought again of how they might have been tracked to the hotel. Had the gunman figured out he was with Kendra? Maybe they'd seen her dog in action and assumed she was with him?

Not just her K9, he realized. But because they'd been in contact. And because her parents had been killed in the same plane crash.

"Keep this safe," Kendra advised, handing it back. "I don't know if you want to part with it, but you don't want it stolen or lost either."

"I will." He turned the coin he'd glued to the keychain over in his fingers. Thinking of the way they'd been found, he inspected it more closely. There was no way a tracking device could be embedded on the coin.

Deep inside his key fob? That seemed extreme. Yet his paranoia was such that he unhooked the Krugerrand coin from his truck's key fob just in case. Granted, they were already at the cabin, so getting rid of it now seemed silly.

Setting the key fob aside, he tucked the Krugerrand into his wallet, then scrubbed his hands over his face. He might be losing it. Maybe this was only about revenge, getting rid of his father and now coming after him because Gunther Volter was still behind bars.

"Hey, it's going to be all right." Kendra's soft hand on his arm had him glancing up at her. Her beautiful blue eyes reflected compassion. She was pretty, not as flashy as Shari had been, but in a wholesome way. "We're going to figure this out. You're the smartest computer whiz on the planet, right?"

"Right." He managed a reluctant smile and did his best to push the despair aside. Mentioning his tech skills made him frown. "That reminds me, I left my team leader in charge of the office in my absence. I just now realized that without my phone, Jake can't contact me if he runs into trouble."

She shrugged. "I'm sure he's smart enough to figure it out, or he wouldn't be your team leader. But if you want to check in with him, you can. I'd wait until tomorrow, though." Kendra glanced around the cabin. "Maybe we'll head into town for you to make that call. Just to be extra cautious."

He couldn't blame her for wanting to stay off-grid. "Okay, that works."

Smoky rose, stretched, then trotted over to stand by the door. Kendra noticed and stood with a rueful smile. "That's my cue to take her outside."

He nodded, watching as she shrugged into her

coat, then headed into the cold. Alone, he dropped his head into his hands.

Both his parents had been brutally murdered, and now someone wanted to make sure he was eliminated too. He appreciated Kendra's support, but keeping her close was likely to get her killed too.

Tomorrow, he'd insist they go their separate ways.

HUNCHING her shoulders against the cold wind, Kendra scanned her surroundings the way Chase had taught her. The snow beyond the area around the SUV remained undisturbed. While that was reassuring, she also knew that anyone with a weapon could fire at them from the safety of the woods.

Handguns weren't as accurate as a rifle for long distances, though. Still, she studied the foliage, searching for an intruder. She was glad she'd turned the SUV around so that the front was facing the driveway in the event they needed to get out of there quickly.

Smoky romped and played, clearly loving the snow. Shaking her head, Kendra called, "Get busy. Come on, Smoky. Get busy!"

Her K9 turned to look at her for a moment, then sniffed the ground to find the perfect spot to do her thing. When Smoky had finished, the dog ran back toward her, curvy tail wagging madly.

Normally, Kendra loved spending time outdoors with her dog, but she needed to get back inside to talk to Dom. The poor guy was still reeling from the information Raine had shared.

"Let's go, Smoky." Kendra turned and trudged back to the front door. "I need you to help cheer Dominic up, okay?"

Smoky brushed past her, going into the warm cabin. Then the K9 stood and shook herself to get rid of the excess snow. Dominic was still sitting in the spot where she'd left him, and he chuckled as he swiped water from his face.

Mission accomplished, she thought with a smile as she shrugged out of her coat and hung it on the hook near the door. When Dom stood, she glanced up at him. His blond hair was tousled as if he'd raked his hands through it. "I wish we had coffee."

"Did you check the freezer?" She headed into the kitchen. "I know when my brother was here last, he left coffee behind."

"Really?" His expression turned hopeful.

She opened the freezer and found a can of coffee. "Here we go." She handed it to him. "Do you always drink coffee all day and into the night?"

"Pretty much." He gratefully took the coffee and crossed to the coffeemaker. "Especially if I'm working late on a project." He shot her a rueful glance. "I've never had a project as important as this, though."

"I hear you." She dropped into the empty chair. "It's been a lot to process."

"Yeah." He filled the coffeemaker, then joined her. "I was thinking we should start by digging into Stuart Ramsey's last few weeks in Jackson Hole. We know Gunther Volter was already in jail by then, and it would be nice to know who hired Ramsey. Was it Theo Le Ruiz or someone else? Seems logical that same person is the one who hired this gunman too."

She nodded thoughtfully. "That makes sense. You mentioned exchanging contact information with the hospice nurse. Any chance we can talk to her again tomorrow?"

"We can try, but I don't think she has anything more to add." He turned to the computer. "I'm sure she told me everything she knows."

"I figure it can't hurt." She drummed her fingers on the table. "She called you on Sunday, right? Just over a week later, a gunman is hot on your trail. If nothing else, we should make sure she's okay."

"True." His eyes widened in alarm. "I hadn't considered the fact that she might be in danger too."

She winced, wishing she hadn't mentioned it. "I'm sure she's fine. For whatever reason, this guy thinks you know something you shouldn't. Maybe he's worried your father spoke about his time prior to being relocated into witness protection."

"Maybe." He rerouted his ISP address again, then pulled up his email. She leaned over to watch as he sent Helen Gingrass a message to stay safe and that he'd like to call her the following day. Dom glanced at her. "Should I call the Denver police?"

She arched a brow. "Denver? I assumed the hospice was in Billings."

"No, Denver." He scowled at the screen. "When the Billings police showed up on my doorstep, they mentioned being contacted by the Denver PD. And the area code of Helen's phone was also from Denver. I know Stuart Ramsey worked in Jackson, then sabotaged the plane in Billings six years ago, but after that, he must have taken the cash and relocated to Colorado."

"Or he moved to Denver from some other town after being diagnosed with cancer." The coffeemaker stopped brewing, so she stood to fill their cups.

"I think it's easier to disappear in a larger town than someplace smaller where everyone knows everyone else." Dom accepted the coffee cup with a smile of thanks. When their fingers brushed, a tingle of awareness danced up her arm. She worked hard to ignore it. This was the wrong time, the wrong place, and Dom was the wrong guy for her.

Just because every single one of her older siblings was now married, or in Trevor's case engaged, didn't mean she needed to do the same. She was only twenty-five, no reason to rush into anything.

Besides, Dominic lived and worked in Billings. Kendra couldn't imagine leaving her family ranch.

Thinking of that, though, along with the gold Krugerrand, made her think of something. "Dom, you mentioned you found the coin in your dad's plane hangar. You're sure other coins aren't hidden someplace in there?"

"I'm sure." Dom sounded certain. "I stayed in my dad's house after he died. I turned the office in the plane hangar into my home office. There's storage in there, too, but I've been through those boxes. I never found any coins. Or anything that would indicate my father had once lived in New Jersey."

She nodded. "We stayed in our parents' home after they died too. Well, technically, my older siblings Maya, Chase, and Jessica moved back to the ranch, giving up their careers and lives to support us younger siblings." Mostly her, Kendra knew. She'd wrestled with guilt over that for months, until Maya and Chase had both told her they were thrilled to be working search and rescue. That this was their life calling, not their previous careers.

Taking their words to heart, she had let go of the guilt. None of them had anticipated losing their parents at such a young age. But they'd pulled together and turned their inheritance into a way to serve their community.

A mission her parents would have been proud of.

And now her siblings were all happily married and engaged, thrilled to bring forward the next generation of Sullivans. Joel and Trina's son, Ben, was the oldest. Chase's son, Eli, was next in line, with Trevor and Bailey's new daughter, Naomi, coming in third. But there would soon be many other Sullivan babies at the ranch. Maya and Doug's son was due on Christmas Day, and Chase and Wynona's daughter was due the second week in January. Jessica and Logan were expecting in late February, and Libby, Shane's wife, was also newly pregnant.

Kendra knew it was silly to feel left out. She was looking forward to helping to care for the new generation of Sullivans.

"We have that in common." Dom's words drew her from her thoughts. "It wasn't easy to live in the house after my dad died, but since I graduated college early and got the job at Data Intelligence Services, I figured I may as well stay."

"We felt the same way." She touched his arm. "I know you might not believe in God and Jesus, but we have taken great comfort in knowing our parents are watching over us in heaven."

"I haven't been to church in years," Dom confessed. "I'm not even sure if my father believed, although he took me to church until I was a teenager. Once I started working, those services were less frequent until they stopped altogether."

She wanted to point out that church alone wasn't enough, but based on what she'd learned about Dom's father, she was surprised he'd attended services at all. The guy had discovered a criminal enterprise, lost his wife, and then been plucked out of New Jersey to live in Billings, Montana. It couldn't have been easy for him to raise a small child alone in a place where he didn't know anyone.

"Here's what I found out while you were outside." Dom tapped the computer screen. "It turns out there is one main charter service in Jackson Hole. And I think it may be the place where Stuart Ramsey worked."

"What makes you say that?"

"Because it's an exclusive, high-priced operation. Something that would appeal to rich people. Their planes are very plush. Check this out." He turned the screen so she could see better. The interior of the plane was fancy, a far cry from what Logan's planes offered. Then again, Logan tended to shuttle hunters around, not rich people.

"Okay, but even if that is the place Ramsey worked, we're not going to be able to figure out who used the service prior to our parents' plane going down."

"Oh, ye of little faith," Dom scoffed. "I've already hacked into their database." His fingers flew across the keyboard. "First of all, I found Stuart Ramsey's name listed as a former employee."

"Wow, you can do that?" She couldn't help being impressed. "How long had Stuart worked there?"

"Eight years." Dom didn't take his eyes off the screen as he worked. "Helen mentioned Stuart had sabotaged my dad's plane for money, and the police mentioned he had gambling debts. I'm more interested in who hired him."

Kendra nodded. He was right, Stuart's motive wasn't as important as the guy who'd hired him. "Still, I'm not sure we'll know which person is guilty just by looking at names on a roster."

Dom shot her a quick look. "It's a place to start. We need to know who is trying to kill me. Well, both of us now," he amended.

She sipped her coffee, watching him work. Smoky snoozed on the floor at her feet. Dom alternated between jotting names on one tab of his computer screen and searching the database for others.

Leaving him to it, Kendra rose and added more

wood to the fireplace. Smoky rose, stretched, and followed her.

Sitting around twiddling her thumbs while Dom worked wasn't easy. Despite drinking coffee at eight in the evening, she yawned.

"Hey, why don't you get some sleep?" Dom suggested.

She turned to face him. "Are you going to get some sleep?"

"No. Not until I have a lead on the guy who hired this gunman." He gestured toward the hallway leading to the bedrooms. "There's no reason for both of us to stay awake. Get some rest, Kendra."

"Not yet." It wasn't that late. After adding one more log to the fire, she joined him back at the table. "Is there something I can do?"

"Not really." He stopped typing for a moment, then turned the screen toward her. "Take a look at these names. Any of them look or sound familiar?"

Resting her chin in her hand, she read through the names. There were only six, and not a single one looked familiar. "No, sorry. What's your thought? To see if any of them have ties to Gunther Volter? Or to South Africa?" She doubted there was a website out there that listed the members of the Randover Royals.

"Yes, exactly." He shrugged and turned the screen back. "I wish I had asked Raine for the name of the company my father worked for as an accountant."

"We can follow up with Raine about that in the morning." She stifled another yawn. "I doubt that company is still in business, though. They'd have gone down after my father testified against Gunther, right?"

"Probably." Dom glanced at her again. "I can't believe they killed my mother to convince my father to keep quiet."

"Very brutal and coldhearted." Especially since the bad guys had intended to kill an innocent three-year-old Dominic too. "I'm sorry. Maybe someday you'll be able to meet your mother's family."

"Doubtful, but that's okay." He sighed and turned his attention back to the screen. A message popped up. "Wow, looks like Helen just got back to me."

"What did she say?" Kendra leaned forward again.

Dom opened the message. Helen agreed to talk, then mentioned how she'd received a South African gold coin from Stuart that she discovered was worth $3,824.

Kendra blinked. Stuart had given Helen a Krugerrand? Was that small gold coin the real reason the gunman wanted to kill Dominic?

6

"I'm surprised to hear Stuart Ramsey gave Helen a Krugerrand." Dominic couldn't tear his gaze from the message on the screen. He pulled the coin he'd always considered to be worthless from his pocket. Apparently, Raine Sullivan was correct about the value of the coin.

"I wonder if the bad guy paid Stuart in Krugerrand to sabotage your dad's plane." Kendra's expression was thoughtful. "Or if he found it lying around in your father's hangar, the way you did."

He lifted his head to stare at her. "That never occurred to me. Although I highly doubt my dad would have left more than one of them fall to the ground." Another idea popped into his head. "Maybe Stuart stole it from a stash he found in my dad's plane."

Kendra nodded. "We need to consider all possibilities. For all we know, there're more Krugerrand lying around in the mountains somewhere."

He grimaced. "If there is, we'll never find it, not after all this time." He didn't really care about the money. He made a decent living at his job and had inherited his father's house after his death. It wasn't as if he needed more. "But now I'm starting to think that maybe these guys are coming after me because they think I have a stash of Krugerrand."

"I don't know about that. Why wouldn't they just search your place?" Kendra's brow furrowed. "Killing you wouldn't help them find it."

Her comment brought another memory to the surface. One that he hadn't thought much about until now. "I think they did search our home. Shortly before my dad's plane went down."

"Really?" Kendra's blue gaze locked on his. "What happened?"

"There was a break-in at our house. I remember my dad was pretty upset about it, even though the Billings police was convinced a couple of kids were responsible. Apparently, there had been other break-ins in another area of the city." He tried to recall the pertinent details. "Our house and hangar are located on the outskirts of town. My dad pointed that out to the police, wondering why the kids would come all the way out by us to steal. The cops told me they believed the kids responsible went to my school. That was why they came out to our place."

"But now you think the break-in was related to the Krugerrand," Kendra said. "Although why would Gunther's guys wait so long to search in the first place?"

"I don't know. I guess that depends on how they found my father's identity and location." He shook his head. "Now that I know my dad was placed in witness protection, I'm trying to figure out how and where he learned to fly small planes. That doesn't seem like a hobby an accountant would have."

"That's a really good question." Kendra bent to stroke a hand over Smoky's fur. "From what I've read, anyone going into witness protection is advised against keeping previous hobbies. If your dad had known how to fly planes before he was relocated to Billings, he never should have used that skill as his source of income."

"Maybe he didn't have a choice?" Dom knew his knee-jerk defense of his father wasn't warranted. "I mean, how else is a single father supposed to support himself and a small kid?"

"I didn't intend to criticize him," she quickly interjected. "I'm sure your dad did his best for you."

He blew out a breath, reminding himself there was a lot about his father he didn't know. Like the fact that they were in witness protection. And that his father's testimony against Gunther Volter had put the man behind bars. "I know you didn't. I'm being overly sensitive about all of this. I don't want to believe my father's decisions caused his death." Not just his father's demise, but Kendra's losing her parents too.

"This isn't your father's fault," Kendra said firmly. "Your dad did the right thing in coming forward. In testifying against Volter. First, he lost his wife, then he gave up the life he knew for you, Dom. I'm sure it wasn't easy for a guy from New Jersey to start over and acclimate to Billings, Montana."

"True." He forced a smile. Kendra was sweet and kind. As much as he'd tried to convince her to head back to the safety of the Sullivan ranch, he was glad she was there with him. "Thanks for saying that."

"It's the truth." She waved a hand. "I'm still not sure why the gunman has come after you now, though. What could they possibly want after all this time?"

"Revenge? Payback for my father testifying against Volter?"

"They could have finished you off six years ago, but they didn't. They chose to come after you now."

He felt like they were going in circles, rehashing the same thing over and over. Maybe this was about the Krugerrand. He didn't want to believe his dad had stolen it, but he was forced to consider anything was possible. Had Krugerrand helped pay for his father's plane? He wasn't sure how the charter business had been funded in the first place.

So many questions without answers. And with his father being gone, Dom wasn't sure he'd ever know the truth.

"Hey, we're going to figure this out." Kendra rested her hand on his arm. The warmth of her fingers seemed to radiate up his extremity. Getting emotionally entangled with Kendra wasn't smart. Much like his former girlfriend, Shari Coffen, she was pretty enough to have any guy she wanted.

She didn't need to settle for a beanpole like him.

"We can ask Helen about the coin tomorrow." Kendra's voice pulled him from his thoughts. If he didn't watch out, he'd get his foolish heart broken all over again. "Stuart may have confided in her about how he received it. I'm leaning toward the theory that Gunther's men paid Stuart with the coins to get rid of your dad."

"Yeah. Maybe." He was still having trouble wrapping his mind around how valuable the coin was. Why would his father have allowed him to keep the gold coin if he knew it was worth so much money?

"We should probably get some sleep." Kendra squeezed his arm, then stood. "I need to take Smoky out one last time."

"Okay." Despite his exhaustion, Dom doubted he'd sleep. Not when his mind was going a million miles an hour.

Everything he thought he knew about himself and his father was a lie. One born out of necessity, but still untrue. Maybe their best option was to meet with the US Marshals office. At the very least, Andrew Levy might be able to answer a few of his questions.

But they wouldn't meet with him here, in the cabin. Dom rose and crossed to the fire. This was the first place he'd felt safe since the initial gunfire had erupted outside the Redwood Motel. They'd used disposable phones, and he'd covered their ISP address to use the computer. He honestly couldn't think of anything else he could do to keep them off-grid.

He headed down the hall and poked his head into the various bedrooms. Kendra should take the master suite. He could make do with the bedroom directly across the hall from the second bathroom.

"It's snowing," Kendra announced when she and Smoky returned. Seeing the snowflakes covering Smoky's fur had him taking a step back to avoid the dog's inevitable shaking.

"Maybe that will help keep the bad guys from finding us." He couldn't help but smile ruefully when Smoky shook the excess water from her fur.

"I took the time to brush the snow off the SUV just in case." Kendra set her damp gloves on the table to dry. "Having fresh snow on the ground will make it easy to see tracks if someone does find us."

He frowned. "Nobody will find us here."

"I hope not." Kendra offered a lopsided smile. "My siblings were all in danger over the past year, and despite their best efforts, they were often found when they should have been safe. At this point, I'd rather be prepared for the worst-case scenario."

"I understand." He gestured toward the bedrooms. "You can have the master suite. I'm going to work for a while yet."

"Work as in performing tasks you do for your day job? Or work on finding information about Stuart Ramsey?"

"Stuart Ramsey. I'm on vacation from the day job. Although at some point, I should reach out to my team leader, Jake, to give him my new number. He's good, but he's relatively new to the company. He's likely to have questions."

"Leave that for tomorrow. You've only been gone a few hours. I'm sure he can hold the fort down for a day or two."

"Yeah." Dom knew part of his concern was just making sure everything was done according to his expectations. He tried not to micromanage his team, but he also wanted to be sure things were done correctly. He tucked his hands into the front pockets of his jeans. "Good night, Kendra."

"Good night." She turned. "Come, Smoky."

Dom watched as Kendra and her K9 went down the hall and into the main bedroom. Reminding himself again that they were friends, allies, and partners in this, nothing more, he turned his attention back to the computer.

He'd work for at least an hour. He needed something, anything they could use to figure out who had targeted him and why.

Revenge for what his father had done? Or something related to the coins? Or something else? No matter what his father had done, Dom was determined to uncover the truth.

Kendra didn't fall asleep as easily as she'd hoped. It wasn't Smoky's gentle snores that kept her awake, it was concern over possibly being found at the cabin.

Dominic knew how to keep their internet access private, but she was worried the bad guys would still find them. How, she wasn't sure. Her role as being the technical support for the ranch was laughable compared to Dominic's abilities.

At some point, Kendra must have drifted off because a low growl woke her. She bolted upright, blinking against the darkness. Smoky's eyes were fixated on the window.

Scrambling from the bed, Kendra slipped her feet into her shoes and padded to the window. Staying to the side, she peered outside, looking for whatever had caught Smoky's attention.

The closed window indicated her K9 hadn't scented anything alarming, but she also knew dogs had better hearing than humans.

For long seconds, she didn't see anything. Had Smoky heard an animal? Maybe a moose or an elk? Bears were hibernating by now, so she didn't think they were a concern.

Then she caught a glimpse of movement through the trees. Narrowing her gaze, she followed the dark shadow's progress. She didn't see any footprints in the snow, but that didn't mean there wasn't someone hiding in the woods.

The shadow that moved between the trees wasn't as tall as a moose or an elk. Then she caught a glimpse of a man's face.

Someone was out there! Kendra spun from the window, mentally berating herself for leaving her weapon in the kitchen. She quickly crossed over to open the door, glancing cautiously up and down the hallway before moving to the kitchen. Dominic was sitting at the table with his head cradled in his hands. Clearly, he'd fallen asleep while working.

The computer was dark, which was a good thing. She didn't want any interior lights to draw the intruder's attention. She grasped Dom's shoulder. "Wake up," she whispered. "Someone's outside."

"What?" Dom lifted his head and blinked his eyes. "Are you sure?"

"Yes, I saw a man out back. We need to make a run for it. Grab your computer." Keeping her head low, she grabbed the gun and tucked it into her waistband. "Let's go."

Dom's expression was grim as he reached for his coat. She slipped into hers, then grabbed her backpack. She couldn't leave without Smoky's food and protective gear. Dom edged up to the window overlooking the front of the property. She joined him, relieved there weren't fresh footprints around the SUV.

Hopefully that meant the vehicle hadn't been tampered with. And there wasn't a moment to lose. "I'll head to the driver's seat. There isn't time to get Smoky in the back. I'll have her get into the back seat. You need to keep your head down, understand?"

He nodded. "I'm ready."

Their only advantage was surprise. The moment they made any noise, the gunman would fire at them. Sending up a quick prayer for safety, she silently opened the front door of the cabin, taking a moment to scan the area. Her main reason for not using the back crate area was to avoid the beeping sound that accompanied the hatch lifting upward. That and her fear that it would take too long to get the back opened and closed again.

She stepped outside, with Dom following. The thick snow muffled the sound of their footsteps. She and Dom opened their respective car doors at the same time. She tossed the backpack into the back, then gave Smoky the hand signal to get inside. The K9 paused for a beat, as she normally didn't go into the car like this, but when Kendra repeated the gesture, Smoky leaped up inside, squeezing through the two front seats to get into the back. Kendra quickly slid in behind the wheel as Dominic folded himself into the passenger seat.

The sound of their car doors closing was loud enough to make her wince. She pressed the start button, hit the wipers to remove the inch of snow covering the windshield, and put the car in gear. Punching the gas, she barreled down the driveway as fast as the snow-covered gravel road would allow. Having the SUV in four-wheel drive helped, but their progress wasn't nearly as quick as she'd have liked.

A crack of gunfire rang out behind them. Kendra

didn't bother to look at the rearview mirror as the back window was still mostly covered in snow. Instead, she focused on keeping the SUV from sliding too much as she navigated the vehicle toward the road.

Another crack of gunfire rang out. Thankfully, she didn't hear any metallic pings indicating they'd been hit. The road was just a few yards ahead. Once they reached the road, she pulled on the steering wheel, making a hard left, then punched the gas again to put as much distance between them and the shooter behind them as possible.

A long silence hung between them. Kendra cranked the heat, hoping the warmth would melt the snow from the rest of the windows.

"How did you know someone was outside the cabin?" Dom asked, breaking the silence.

"Smoky woke me." Using the rearview mirror, she eyed her K9 stretched out in the back seat. Smoky was taking advantage of the extra space. Kendra would rather have the dog safely tucked into the crate area, but that would have to wait until later. No way was she stopping anytime soon. "Smoky growled at something she heard outside. I thought at first it was an animal, but then I saw a man moving between the trees. That's when I came to find you."

"Smoky is amazing, but I don't understand how

we were found." Dominic rubbed the back of his neck. "We didn't rent the cabin through legal channels. We used our phones and the internet, but rerouting the server should have worked."

"I don't know what to tell you." She hit both defrost buttons to help melt the remaining snow clinging to the front and rear windows. "I'm just glad Smoky alerted me in time so we could get away."

"Yeah." Dom frowned. "Kendra, this isn't good. If the guys tracking us have some sort of computer guru on their payroll, then we'll have to go completely off-grid. And that means not using any phones or computer access."

She glanced at him, then eyed the rearview mirror. Seeing nothing on the road behind them, she tried to relax. "If that's our only option, then that's what we'll do."

"I don't want to give up on searching for the truth." Dom's expression was grim. "How are we going to figure out who's after us if we call off the investigation?"

She understood his concern. "We can leave the investigating to my family. My sister-in-law Raine and my brother-in-law Griff can do the legwork."

"Then they'll be in danger." Dom shook his head. "I don't like it. Maybe I didn't do a good enough job of rerouting the server."

Since she had no idea exactly how he'd accomplished that feat, despite watching him in action, she didn't know what to say. She didn't want her family in danger, either, especially since there were several pregnant women on the ranch. But at the same time, she hated to admit they might be in over their heads. "As cops or, in Raine's case, a former cop, they understand and accept the risk of danger."

"I still don't like it," he repeated. "I have another way I can try to hide our electronic trail. It's more complicated than the method I used before. But first, we need a place with internet access."

She sighed and let it go. For now. It was only a matter of time before she was forced to call on her siblings for help. The way she'd promised her oldest brother, Chase. Yet that didn't mean she was going to wake them up at this hour. She grimaced and tapped the clock on the dashboard. "It's only quarter past four in the morning. Too early for any of the breakfast cafés or coffee shops to be open."

"Maybe we should head back to Greybull." Dom shifted in his seat to grab the computer. "I can try to find another rental property."

"Hold off on that for now." She glanced at the rearview mirror to make sure there were still no cars behind them. "Did you learn anything new before you fell asleep?"

"I was able to find the last three charter flights

that landed in the hangar where Stuart Ramsey worked, all a week before he left his job in Jackson." Dominic rubbed his neck again. "I can't believe I fell asleep. I only intended to rest my eyes as the screen kept getting blurry. I'm still getting used to my new contact lenses. I thought they were the problem. Turns out, I was exhausted. Sleeping bent over like that has given me a serious crick in my neck."

"New contact lenses?" she echoed.

"Yeah, glasses are a pain. They fog up in the cold." He waved a hand. "Never mind. The important part is that I was able to track down the charter flights."

She nodded. "You're thinking one of those charter flights is the guy who paid Stuart to sabotage your dad's plane?"

"I figured it couldn't hurt to look into them as potential suspects." He sighed. "I didn't get a chance to dig into their backgrounds, though."

"It's a place to start." She was impressed he'd thought of it. Taking several turns, Kendra wound her way through town, backtracking often enough to hopefully avoid being seen by the gunman. As they wasted time, she debated staying in Cody or heading to Greybull. In her humble opinion, there were more motel and rental options available to them in Cody.

And the city was slightly closer to the ranch than Greybull.

The minutes ticked by with excruciating slowness. A glance at the fuel gauge had her turning at the next intersection.

"We should get some gas, then find a breakfast café." She drove down the brightly lit and Christmasy-decorated main thoroughfare. "Maybe one of them will be open at five or five thirty."

"Okay with me." Dom shifted the computer so he could dig in the front pocket of his jeans. "I have cash for gas."

"I do too. But we'll need some for breakfast too." She pulled into the next gas station, then parked alongside the building when she realized it wasn't open yet either. After a moment's hesitation, she decided to kill the lights but left the engine running. It was too cold to keep the car shut down for long. "Okay, tell me about those charter flights that landed in the hangar where Stuart Ramsey worked."

"They're all men ranging in age from mid-thirties to early sixties." He opened the laptop and turned the screen so she could see. "In age order, their names are Timothy Platt age thirty-five, Lamar Mortenson age forty-nine, and Ian Bartoli age sixty-two."

"None of those names sounds at all familiar."

Not that Kendra had necessarily expected to recognize the guy who'd hired Stuart Ramsey to kill Dom's father and her parents. "I would lean toward one of the older guys."

"I agree, although all three should be vetted regardless." He sighed. "In all fairness, they could be innocent. We don't know for sure that someone chartering a plane from that hangar is involved. Could be one of them learned Stuart was in debt from gambling, making him an easy target for the job."

"True." And yet another reason to ask Raine, Doug, or Griff to lead the investigation. "I can't imagine being in debt is enough to convince someone to ruthlessly sabotage a plane, killing everyone on board."

"Yeah, it's a little crazy." Dom frowned. "Maybe the cartel threatened him in some way if he didn't agree to help."

"Maybe." In her mind, gambling alone didn't equate to agreeing to committing murder. "Raine didn't mention gambling as something the South African cartel was involved in. Just gold, gemstones, and drugs."

"I keep wondering if my dad stole the Krugerrand from the cartel." Dom stared out at the dark parking lot. "He may have sold a bunch of the coins to pay for the plane."

"Gunther Volter could have paid your father in Krugerrand," she pointed out. "Maybe that's how he had his fellow cartel members pay Stuart too."

Dom shrugged but didn't say anything. She could tell he was torn between wanting to defend his father's innocence while also considering his father's culpability. Kendra realized she and her siblings were the fortunate ones in this tragedy. Their parents had been killed through no fault of their own. Not that Gary Lakeland had deserved to die, but if he had done something to let the cartel track him to Billings, then he was partially responsible for leaving Dominic an orphan.

The streets were dark and empty, but when she caught a glimpse of headlights coming toward them, she instinctively killed the engine. At her sudden movement, Dominic glanced over.

"What's wrong?"

She pointed to the lights growing brighter with every passing second. "Sink down in the front seat as low as possible," she whispered.

With his height, that wasn't an easy task. She scooted down, hugging the driver's side door, giving him room to bend over the center console.

"Who do you think is out there?" he asked.

"I don't know." She lifted her head just enough to look over the edge of the dashboard. Then she sank back down again. "It looks like a large truck.

Similar to the one that passed me on the road back in Greybull."

"The shooter?" Now Dominic lifted his head to see better. "He's out there looking for us?"

Kendra didn't know if the truck belonged to the shooter or not. She grabbed the front of Dom's jacket, tugging him down. The lights outside grew so bright she found herself holding her breath, anticipating the SUV would be slammed with bullets any second.

She desperately wanted the truck to assume the SUV was empty and move on. But when the lights didn't fade away, she pulled her weapon from her waistband, preparing for the worst.

If they were going to die today, she would do her best to make sure she took the gunman down with them.

7

———————

Despite his height, Dom scrunched down in the seat as much as possible. He wasn't sure the headlights belonged to the shooter, but he understood Kendra's concern. And when he glimpsed the gun in her hand, his blood ran cold. They were sitting ducks out there. If the gunman behind the wheel intended to open fire, their chance of getting out alive was next to nothing.

Despair hit hard. If they died there today, they'd never know the truth about who this guy was or why he'd come after them. Or how they kept getting found. And worse, Kendra would lose her life because of him.

"I'm sorry," he whispered.

"Not your fault," she whispered back. "If he opens fire, I'll do my best to take him down."

He was tempted to take the gun from her, to do the deed himself, but knew she was likely a better shot than he was. He was about to risk a glance over the steering wheel when he noticed the lights weren't as bright as they had been. He frowned, trying to imagine what might have been happening. The lights hadn't abruptly shut off, indicating the gunman was getting out of the truck to investigate. The brightness slowly faded as if the vehicle was driving away.

Still, he didn't move. His face was inches from Kendra's. Another irrational thought hit. He didn't want to die without kissing her.

Ridiculous to be thinking of such a thing at a time like that. Then again, he'd never faced death like this before. He'd lost his father, but that was different.

Kendra wiggled around to peer up over the dashboard. After a moment, she pushed herself all the way up. "The truck is gone."

"Good." Dom unfolded himself from his cramped position. Then he grabbed Kendra's hand. "Please drop me off and head home to the ranch. I can't stand the thought of this guy killing you."

"I can't stand the idea of this guy killing you either." She held his gaze, her fingers tightening around his. "I mean it, Dominic. I won't leave you to face this guy alone."

He tried to come up with an argument that would change her mind. He was the real target here, not her. Although maybe by now this guy wouldn't be satisfied unless he took them both out of the picture.

"Your father and my parents were ruthlessly murdered," Kendra spoke in a low, soft voice. "We're in this together. I have a feeling that it will take both of us to uncover the truth." She glanced to the back seat where Smoky was still stretched out asleep. "All three of us," she amended.

He was touched by her words. Kendra was sweet, kind, and honorable. As he struggled to find the words to tell her how much she meant to him, she released his hand to cup his cheek. Then she leaned in for a kiss.

The brief caress of her mouth against his fried his brain cells. He savored her sweetness, then abruptly broke away when the gas station lights flipped on, bathing them in light.

"I—uh." He had no clue what to say. He felt like he was in high school again, kissing his girlfriend in the front seat of his truck. Although back then, he would have been the one behind the wheel. Kendra deserved better.

Yet she was the one who'd kissed him. Not the other way around.

"Um . . ." He had no idea what to say.

"I guess we can get gas now." A smile tugged at the corners of her mouth. She appeared amused by his discomfort. "But let's just wait another few minutes. I want to be sure that truck doesn't turn around and come back."

The truck. He forced himself to focus on the threat of danger. Not on how much he wanted to kiss Kendra again. "You really think the gunman is driving around searching for us?"

She shrugged. "Why not? For all we know, the guy has my license plate number. If so, we need to rent a vehicle. Or swap license plates with another car."

"Swapping plates is against the law." As soon as he uttered the words, he realized how ridiculous they sounded. Better to break the law and remain alive than continue driving around with a target on their back. "But if you think we should make a swap, I'll figure out a way to get it done."

"Getting a rental might be better, only because the crate area of the SUV may be too noticeable." She frowned, then started the car. "Unfortunately, the Sullivan family is well known in the area. Everyone knows we have crates and special features built into our SUVs for our K9s."

He nodded in understanding. The crate area was distinctive and could be seen from a distance. "Whatever you think is best."

She shifted into gear and pulled away from the side of the building. "We'll fill up with gas first since the rental agencies won't be open for several hours. Then we'll figure out where to go from here."

He didn't argue. His expertise was technology, not figuring out how to hide from a gunman who seemed to find them no matter where they went.

Was it possible this guy had similar computer hacking skills that he did? Dominic knew his knowledge wasn't unique. A lot of people could do what he did.

The thought nagged at him as Kendra pulled up to a gas pump. He pushed out of the passenger seat, relieved for the opportunity to stretch his legs. Hunching his shoulders against the cold, he strode into the station/convenience store to prepay. Removing a couple of twenty-dollar bills from his pocket, he slid them across the counter. "Please release pump number four."

"Got it." The clerk pushed a button. "Go ahead."

Dom quickly headed back outside. Kendra was already out of the vehicle with the gas nozzle tucked into her fuel tank. He stepped forward. "I'll do this. Get back inside where it's warm."

She shrugged. "Thanks, I'll let Smoky out."

He watched as she told the fluffy dog to get busy. Then he grinned as the K9 jumped into the snowbank, seemingly eager to romp and play.

Maybe he should get a dog once this nightmare was over. He worked from home most of the time, so there was no reason he shouldn't have a pet.

When the gas tank was full, he replaced the nozzle and headed back inside. Kendra and Smoky accompanied him.

"Do you have gas station video surveillance?" Kendra asked.

The clerk frowned. "Yeah, but you don't look like a Cody police officer."

"I'm not, but I can ask them to head over here if necessary. Burt Jones and Sergeant Tom Howell are friends of the Sullivan family." Kendra gestured to the pumps outside. "Does your camera record all night? Or just during the hours you're open? We're interested in seeing the video from the past thirty minutes or so."

"It's on all night." The clerk pushed the couple dollars in change for the gas toward Dominic. "But I'm not supposed to give the video out to anyone but the police."

"Great, I'll call them." Kendra reached into her pocket for her phone.

"Okay, okay." The clerk threw up his hands. "Since you're a Sullivan, I'll show you the video."

Dom was surprised the guy gave in to Kendra's request. Apparently, her family was next to royalty in this city. He doubted the gunman had taken the

Sullivan notoriety into the equation when he'd targeted them.

"Here's the video." The clerk turned the screen so they could see it. He was impressed the video was so readily available. "You want to see the past thirty minutes or so, right?"

"Correct." Kendra leaned in as the clerk backed up the video and hit play.

"Do you mind if I manipulate the controls?" Dom didn't wait for the clerk to respond as he took over the keyboard. He hit the fast-forward button until the headlights came onto the screen. Then he slowed the tape, watching as the large dark truck came into view.

"No front license plate," Kendra murmured. "They're not required, but I had hoped that there might be one."

He continued watching the truck as it slowed to a crawl. Clearly, the truck had noticed the SUV parked along the building. If not for Kendra forcing them down out of sight, the guy may have opened fire. Then the truck increased its speed, continuing down the road. The angle wasn't great, so he couldn't see a rear license plate.

"It's a GMC Sierra pickup truck." He released the controls back to the gas station clerk. "I guess that's more than what we knew before."

"Yeah." Kendra smiled at the clerk. "Thanks for sharing that with us."

"No problem." The guy furtively glanced around as if his boss might show up at any moment. Then he added, "Your brother Joel and his K9 helped find my cousin's kid a few months ago. Your family does a lot for our community. I figure this is the least I can do in return."

"We appreciate your help very much. Thanks again for allowing us to see the video." Kendra turned toward Dominic. "Let's get out of here and find a place to get breakfast. And we should probably let the Cody police know about the make and model of the truck. The officers on patrol can help keep an eye out for it."

"Okay." He gave the clerk a nod. "Thank you."

Moments later, they were settled in the SUV. This time, Kendra placed Smoky in the crate area. It occurred to Dominic that if the dog had been back there earlier, the gunman may have realized they were hiding inside.

The near miss hit him hard. As if sensing his mood, Kendra reached over to touch his arm. "God is watching over us, Dom. We'll be okay."

"You really believe that." It wasn't a question. He could tell by the sincere and intense look in her eyes that she did. "If that's the case, then why did your parents have to die in that plane crash?"

She started the car and pulled out of the gas station parking lot. "Losing my parents was difficult, but we always took heart in knowing they were together in heaven looking down on us. The truth is, they're in a better place where there is no pain, fear, worry, or evil men with guns." Kendra grimaced. "I'm not explaining this well, but God put us here on earth to follow His word. To help others, especially those in need. And maybe He brought you and I together to find the bad guys who took my parents and your father, bringing them to justice."

He stared up at the dark sky. Maybe she was right, at least about their being together for justice.

Yet he also didn't want anything bad to happen to Kendra. He opened his heart and prayed that whatever happened in the next day or two, that God would spare Kendra's life.

No matter what happened to him.

KENDRA WASN'T sure she'd convinced Dominic of God's love and protection and hoped that maybe once this was over, she could bring Dominic to church with her family. Christmas was only a few weeks away, and she knew he didn't have any other family to see over the holiday.

Did Dominic get lonely? She had never been

alone in her entire life, having eight older siblings. Her life had always been full of chaos, but at the same time, she'd always known that any one of her siblings would have dropped everything to help her when needed.

Like now. As she drove through Cody, taking side streets to avoid the main thoroughfares, she knew it was time to call for reinforcements. She and Dom needed help, and heading to the ranch, putting pregnant women and children in danger, wasn't an option.

She didn't want to admit failure, yet she had promised Chase she'd ask for help if things got dicey. Seeing that truck on the gas station video slowing as it passed by the SUV where they'd been hiding was sobering.

"I don't think we should return to the Hitching Post," Dom said, breaking into her thoughts. "We need a different place to go."

"I agree." She forced a reassuring smile. "There's a place called Sunny Side Up Café. I think they open early."

"Works for me." Dom glanced back to where Smoky sat in the crate area. "After we eat, we need to rent a fresh car. You're right about the crate being noticeable."

"I agree." She glanced at him. "The only problem with renting a car is leaving a paper trail."

"I know." He shifted in the seat. "I was thinking I could contact my team lead, Jake. He can rent it under his name, listing me as the driver."

Kendra frowned. "I'm not sure I want to drag other innocent people into this."

"I don't either, but if it helps keep us under the radar, then I'm willing to ask him." Dominic peered out the window. "Is that the Sunny Side Up Café over there?"

"Yes." She was relieved to see the lights were on inside. Still, she didn't go directly to the café. Turning left, she headed into a well-established neighborhood. Considering how close they'd come to being found in the SUV earlier, she thought it better to park somewhere else and walk to the café.

Not that two people and a dog were invisible. She hoped Smoky's light fur would blend in with the snow. And she doubted the gunmen would expect them to be on foot. She imagined they were still driving around, searching for the SUV.

Spying a familiar address, she quickly stopped.

"Do you know the family that lives here?" Dom frowned as she pulled up alongside the curb and backed into the driveway of a house that was completely dark.

"I do, yes. The owner is a friend of my brother Joel. His name is Grady McFarland." She gnawed on her lower lip. "I'm not sure if he's home. I know he travels a lot for work." She wasn't sure exactly what Grady did, but she knew he was rarely at home. "I'm sure he won't mind if we borrow his driveway." She parked well off to the side so she wouldn't block him in. As she threw the gearshift into park and killed the engine, she wondered if Grady would mind if they used the place as a hideout if he wasn't home. Joel had used it in the past, and Grady hadn't minded. She made a mental note to call Joel after breakfast to ask for Grady's contact information. For now, she figured Grady would recognize the SUV as belonging to one of the Sullivans. "We'll walk to the café from here."

"Okay." Dom looked surprised by her decision but didn't argue. "Whatever you think is best."

She opened the back hatch for Smoky, then walked around to grab the backpack from the back seat. She had enough food for Smoky to last another day, but after that, she'd need to replenish her supplies.

Shoving that problem aside for the moment, she shut the car door and closed the back hatch. "Come, Smoky."

Her K9 trotted to her side, appearing eager to get to work. Too bad she didn't have a way to track the gunman. Her K9 would alert on gunpowder and gun oil, but it would be impossible to track the guy while he was driving around in the GMC truck.

If he was on foot, though, the way they were, that would be different. Kendra was certain Smoky would alert her to the scent of the gunman.

Dominic carried the laptop tucked under his arm as they made their way through the neighborhood. The café was farther than she'd anticipated. She shivered when the cold northerly wind slapped her in the face.

"Stick close to me." Dom looped his arm around her shoulders, pulling her toward his side. She noticed he'd shortened his stride so she could keep up with him. "We'll be there soon."

"I know." She appreciated his efforts to warm her. If things were different, she'd enjoy walking with Dom and Smoky. Reminding herself that Dom lived in Billings, she pushed the thought of spending time with him once this was over, away. "Once we reach the café, we'll call the Cody police first to let them know the truck is for sure a dark GMC Sierra pickup truck. Then we'll call my family."

"Your family?" He frowned. "I thought you didn't want to drag other innocent people into this?"

"I don't, but we're going to need help." She sighed. "Especially since we don't know how this guy keeps finding us."

"I told you I have another plan to hide our internet connection. If we can find a place to stay, we should be safe."

She didn't respond as a few of the houses around them had lights on now, indicating the occupants were getting ready to start their day. There would be more cars on the roads too as people headed to work.

Would that help hide them? Or make it harder for her and Dom to spot the gunman? Both were distinct possibilities.

"Kendra, you mentioned several of your sisters and sisters-in-law are pregnant. And there are kids at the ranch too." Dom frowned down at her. "It's bad enough you're in danger. I'd rather not drag any of your family members into the line of fire."

"I know." She was torn between wanting more support and keeping her family out of this. "We'll start with the local police and go from there. Maybe Raine has additional information for us."

"She'll probably want me to meet with Marshal Andrew Levy," Dom muttered. "Not sure I'm in agreement with that plan."

"We'll have to meet with him sooner or later. Our attempts to stay off the radar haven't worked as well as we'd hoped." She gestured to the lights ahead. "There's the café. I'm starving."

"Me too." Dom didn't say anything more as they

cut through the back parking lot, then went to the front of the café to head inside.

Grateful for the warmth, she stood for a moment, then gestured toward a table in the back. "That's a good spot."

"Works for me." He glanced at Smoky. "I hope they don't mind your dog."

"They won't." She wasn't worried about that. She tossed the backpack in first, then slid into the booth. Dom dropped onto the bench seat across from her. Smoky crawled beneath the table, resting her head between her front paws.

"Good girl," she praised, smoothing a hand over Smoky's soft fur. "You'll get to eat soon, too, okay?"

An older woman who already looked tired, despite the early hour, brought menus and water. "Coffee?"

"Yes, please," she and Dom answered at the same time.

The woman cracked a smile, glanced at Smoky, then fetched their coffee. Kendra added cream to hers, before sipping gratefully.

Once they'd placed their orders, she pulled out her phone. "Time to call the Cody police."

Dom arched a brow. "You have their non-emergency number memorized?"

She nodded. "What can I say? We talk to the local police on a regular basis. Especially over this past year." She listened, waiting for the dispatcher to pick up. "This is Kendra Sullivan. I'd like to speak with one of the officers on duty. We're safe now," she quickly added. "But we have new information related to the gunman who took shots at us outside the Elk Lodge."

"One moment please." The dispatcher put Kendra on hold. Ten seconds later, another voice came over the line. "Kendra? This is Tom Howell. What's this about a gunman?"

Swallowing a sigh, she filled Sergent Howell in on the events over the past twelve hours. "Burt Jones responded to the shooting outside the Elk Lodge. We now know for sure the gunman is driving a dark-colored GMC Sierra pickup truck. Unfortunately, we don't have a license plate."

"Where are you now?" Howell asked. "I've gotten a few interesting calls about you and Dominic Lakeland. Specifically from the US Marshals office."

A chill that had nothing to do with the cold weather outside snaked down her spine. She caught Dominic's gaze. "Who from the marshals office called you, and what did he or she want?"

"Andrew Levy and he wanted to know if you and Dominic Lakeland were here in Cody," Howell explained.

"Andrew Levy?" She repeated the name for Dom's benefit. "What did you tell him?"

"I answered honestly that I hadn't seen you or a man by the name of Dominic Lakeland," Tom assured her. "I tried your cell phone but didn't get an answer."

"That's because we don't have our regular phones." Her mind whirled with possibilities. How had Andrew Levy narrowed his search for them to Cody, Wyoming? Why not assume they were in Billings, Montana? "Don't tell Andrew Levy anything about us. We're not sure we can trust him."

"You don't trust the US Marshals?" Tom's voice rose incredulously. "What have you gotten yourself into?"

"We're in danger, and whoever is after us has the resources to find us despite our efforts to stay off the grid." Dom's expression turned grim as she spoke. "This all started at the Redwood Motel in Greybull. From there, we were followed here to Cody. The man in the GMC Sierra truck has fired at us multiple times, and we have reason to believe he's still out there searching for us."

Tom sighed loudly. "Do Maya and Chase know about this?"

"Yes, I spoke to Chase." She didn't mention that was hours ago or that their situation had changed for the worst since then. "Please don't let Marshal Levy know we're in the area. We're waiting for Raine to give us some inside information on whether we can trust him or not."

Tom didn't know everything about what Raine and Justin had been through a few months ago, but that didn't stop him from saying, "I won't. You've got my word on that."

"Thanks, Tom." A wave of relief hit hard. "I appreciate that. Will you please ask your officers to be on the lookout for a dark GMC Sierra?"

"I will, but I'm running a list of GMC Sierra's registered in the county and there are just over a dozen of them. Half are dark colors." He was sounding testy again. "I can't have all the drivers treated like suspects."

She winced. "I know that. I highly doubt the driver of the truck is from this area. He's likely from out of town."

"Even worse, but I promise my officers will keep their eyes open for trouble." There was a pause, then he asked, "Do you have anything else?"

"No, but thanks, Tom. We'll be in touch." She lowered the phone. "Sounds like narrowing the search to a GMC Sierra won't help."

"Yeah, I'm getting that," Dom agreed. He set the laptop on the table and connected to the free internet. "I think we call the hospice nurse, Helen Gingrass, next."

"It's a little early," she protested.

"She works day shift." He glanced at the early hour, then shrugged. "Figure we might catch her before she heads to work."

"Unless today is her day off." Kendra sat back in the booth. "Worst case, you can leave a message."

Of course, Helen didn't answer, so he identified himself and then asked for a call back. Less than two minutes later, his phone rang.

"That was fast." He grinned and answered. "Helen, is that you?" When the color leeched from his face, she leaned forward in concern. "I'm so sorry. I had no idea." There was a pause, then he said, "I understand. Thank you for letting me know."

"Know what?" She stared at him as he lowered the device. "What happened?"

"Helen Gingrass was killed in a car crash late last night." Dom appeared stunned. "That was her daughter. It was a hit-and-run. The police are still investigating, but they don't have many leads."

A hit-and-run? Kendra shivered again as the news of Helen's death sank deep. First Stuart Ramsey confessed to murder to Helen, then she notifies Dominic and the police. Now she's dead?

Kendra wasn't a cop, but she felt certain Helen's death was no accident. It was far more likely that whoever had hired Stuart Ramsey six years ago was tying up loose ends.

8

———————

My mother died in a car crash. She's dead. The woman's words from the recent phone call ricocheted through Dom's mind as he stared at the empty seats within the restaurant. He couldn't believe the hospice nurse was gone. And he found the timing of the poor woman's death suspicious. Had the crash been accidental or intentional? Had the hospice nurse been brutally murdered?

If so, why? Because she'd passed along Stuart Ramsey's confession? Or because she was given a Krugerrand? It seemed ludicrous that she would have been killed over a measly four thousand dollars. Not that other innocent victims hadn't been killed for less. He hadn't wanted to press the distraught daughter, but he was curious about whether Helen had the Krugerrand coin in her possession at the scene of the crash. Or if it had been stolen.

"Hey, it's not your fault." Kendra's low voice managed to penetrate his thoughts. He shifted his gaze to her.

"It feels like it." He took a sip of his coffee. "Do you think Helen's death was a random event?"

"No." Kendra's expression turned grim. "I think the fact that she took Stuart's confession put her on the gunman's radar."

Dom wasn't sure if he should be relieved or upset that his thoughts and Kendra's were aligned. "Okay, but if that's the case, how did the gunman get from here, to Denver, and back here so quickly?"

Her brow furrowed. "That would be impossible. Denver is seven hours from here. Round trip would be fourteen. There's no way the same gunman is responsible for shooting at us and causing Helen's crash."

He grimaced. "That means there are several gunmen after us."

"At least two of them," Kendra agreed.

"I feel bad for Helen's daughter." He stopped talking when their server headed toward them with two plates of food. His appetite had been ruined, but he forced a smile as she placed their plates on the table. "Thank you."

"Looks great." Kendra's smile didn't reach her eyes either. "Thanks."

He picked up his fork, then dropped it when Kendra stretched her hand across the table. Belatedly remembering she always said grace, he took her hand in his.

"Dear Lord Jesus, please bless this food we are about to eat. We ask You to keep Helen's family in Your loving arms, offering them comfort despite their loss. And, Lord, please keep us safe in Your care. Amen."

"Amen." The response came without conscious thought, and he found himself thinking about what Kendra had said about her parents being together in heaven. He hadn't thought much about his own death until recent events. Now that he had faced the gunman several times, he realized he wanted eternal life for himself too. He continued to hold Kendra's hand for a long moment. "Thank you, Kendra. I know I have a lot to learn when it comes to prayer."

Hope bloomed in her blue eyes. "I would be happy to help you with that, Dominic. Maybe once the danger is over, you'll consider attending church services with my family."

The distance between Billings and Cody was an hour and forty-five minutes on a good day, depending on the weather, yet that didn't seem too insurmountable. He nodded and forced himself to release her hand. "Thanks. I'd like that."

Kendra's smile was genuine, and there was no denying her prayer had lightened his despair. If Helen Gingrass was a believer, she was in a better place now. Like Kendra's parents.

And his own? He wasn't sure but decided to remain hopeful that they were together again.

His omelet and breakfast potatoes tasted great. His appetite had returned, which was a good thing. He ate quickly, realizing he needed fuel to face whatever lay ahead.

He finished his coffee, glad when their server quickly came to provide a refill.

"I'd like to call my sister-in-law Raine and maybe talk to my brother-in-law Griff too," Kendra said, once they were alone. "Helen's unexpected death changes things. We need law enforcement's help on this."

He tried to read her expression. "You're thinking these guys are getting desperate."

"Yep. And that they're getting rid of all the loose ends." She cradled her mug in her hands. "You and I are the biggest loose ends of all."

Dom had wanted her to go back to the safety of the ranch, but now that Helen was dead, he realized that wouldn't work. If they were loose ends, Kendra would be targeted regardless of where she was.

"I agree it's time to call Raine and Griff." If a former US Marshal and current FBI agent couldn't figure this out, they were sunk. "Maybe they can help put the puzzle pieces together."

"It's almost six now. Not too early, especially since Justin is usually the first one out to the stable each morning to care for the horses." She pulled her phone from her pocket and made the call.

"Raine? It's Kendra. We need your help, Griff's too." He listened as Kendra explained the events that had taken place over the past several hours. "I wish I knew how we were found at the rental property since we didn't even pay to stay there. Dominic thinks maybe he didn't reroute our ISP address as well as he'd thought."

Dom grimaced, hating the fact that he'd failed to keep them safe. Thank goodness for Smoky who had alerted them to the danger. He leaned back to look at the K9 lying at their feet. The dog was so quiet he didn't even know she was there.

"The only way we'll meet with Andrew Levy is if someone is with us," Kendra said firmly. "Whoever hired these guys has some major resources. Not only have we been dodging the gunman here in town, but we suspect the hospice nurse who took Stuart Ramsey's confession was murdered last night in Denver too."

Kendra listened for a long minute. Feeling his gaze, she sent him a reassuring smile.

"Okay, that sounds good. Please bring extra supplies for Smoky, okay? We're at the Sunny Side Up Café. Oh, that reminds me. Ask Justin or Joel if we can stay at Grady McFarland's place for the next several hours. We left our SUV parked in his driveway and walked to the café."

Another pause as Kendra listened. Their server refilled their cups, then hurried away as customers began filling the restaurant. Even at this early hour, people were out and about. Dom scanned the faces of the newcomers, hoping the gunman wasn't hiding in plain sight.

"Thanks, Raine. Appreciate your help." Kendra pocketed the phone. "Raine and Griff are on their way. And I have a feeling Chase will accompany them."

"Great." He forced a smile, but deep down, he was worried that associating with him would get Kendra's family killed. Law enforcement or not, bullets could strike at any time. "I hope they can help us figure out who these guys are."

"They will. And Raine agreed that we shouldn't meet with Levy alone." She eyed the restaurant. "Looks like the place is getting busy." Kendra drained her coffee, then rummaged in her backpack. "I'll feed Smoky, but if the tables fill up, we may need to head back to Grady's to wait for my family."

"Whatever you think is best." He was hardly in a position to argue.

Kendra dumped her water glass into a collapsible bowl. He pushed his over too. With a grateful smile, she added his water to the bowl, then set it down. Smoky didn't move toward the water, but the K9's amber eyes were locked on Kendra.

After she filled another collapsible bowl with food, Kendra set that down on the floor too. Smoky still didn't move. Only when Kendra said, "Come get it," did the dog crawl out from beneath the table and begin to eat.

He wondered how many hours of training it had taken for Smoky to respond like that. He searched the faces of the restaurant patrons again. He'd felt safer when the place had been empty. Now he was seeing a potential gunman everywhere he looked. Granted, there were a few older patrons that weren't likely suspects, but that didn't make him feel any better.

"When Smoky is finished eating, we'll head out." Kendra had noticed his discomfort. "I feel exposed here too."

"What about your family?" He dug for some cash, only to frown when he realized Kendra had beaten him to it.

"We'll call them when we're in the SUV." She shrugged, then smiled as their server set their tab on the edge of the table. "They'll understand."

"Okay." He set his empty coffee cup aside and stood. "May as well make use of the restrooms while we're here."

"Go ahead." She waved a hand. "I'll wait for Smoky to finish."

Ten minutes later, they were back outside with Smoky trotting between them. He scanned the lot, noticing two large trucks. One was light in color, but the other was dark. It wasn't a GMC Sierra, but he gestured toward it anyway. "What do you think?"

"We're fine." Kendra nodded at her K9 who had her head up and was sniffing the air with interest. "Smoky would growl if she scented the gunman."

He shrugged, hoping she was right. The warning niggle along the back of his neck didn't get any better despite being outside. He was still on edge, expecting the worst.

As they headed back toward Grady McFarland's house, he knew the feeling wouldn't go away until they had the gunman behind bars and he knew for certain Kendra and her family were safe.

The last thing he wanted was for anyone else to get hurt.

Dom's shoulders were tense as he hovered beside her. Kendra glanced up at his chiseled features. Their brief kiss flashed in her mind, but she ruthlessly shoved the memory aside.

Dom didn't live in Wyoming, and she wasn't moving off the ranch. Not when there was a new generation of Sullivans soon to be joining the family. They'd always be friends.

Nothing more.

She couldn't blame Dominic for being overly paranoid. She shared his concern about the gunman showing up again. The only good news was that reinforcements were on the way.

"There's a truck coming." Dom grabbed her arm, tugging her back from the road. She bent to make sure Smoky stayed at her side. They stayed in the shadows, watching as the large truck rolled past. When she realized it wasn't a GMC Sierra, the tension leeched from her body.

"We're okay." She forced a reassuring smile. "Grady's home is just six blocks away."

"I know." Dom hadn't relaxed one iota. She knew he was battling guilt over Helen Gingrass's death. It wasn't his fault, but she understood why he felt bad. Maybe if Helen had just kept silent about Stuart's confession, she'd still be alive.

There was no point in thinking that way. Helen was an honorable person, and Kendra gave her credit for doing the right thing, alerting the authorities about Stuart's confession.

The sky remained dark as they walked. Sunrise was still an hour away, and she wanted to be safe inside Grady's house by then. She told Smoky to get busy, and the dog didn't hesitate to make use of a snow-covered area of grass. Kendra quickly cleaned up after her dog, tossing the waste into a nearby garbage can.

A moment later, another pair of headlights lit up the sky. There were no hiding spots nearby this time. Dom wrapped his arm around her, as if that alone would save them from being shot. Thankfully, the driver of the vehicle didn't slow down, which was reassuring.

"I don't know how people live like this," Dom said in a low voice. "Constantly looking over their shoulder? There's no amount of money on the planet for that."

"Desperate people do desperate things." She watched Smoky sniffing along the ground. "We'll get through this."

"I hope so." He didn't sound convinced. Even once they reached Grady's house, Dom didn't relax.

"Still no lights on." Kendra went up to peer through the windows. While it was possible Grady was sleeping in, she didn't think he was home.

"You're not planning to break in, are you?" Dom asked.

"Joel and Justin are friends of his, they went to high school together." She turned and walked to the attached garage. There was a keypad there. She pulled out her phone and made another call. "Hey, Raine, can Justin give me the code for Grady's place?" She punched in the digits. The garage door slowly rose. "We left the restaurant; the place was getting busy."

"We're on the way, but it's going to take us time to get there," Raine told her. "Justin says to make yourself at home. Grady won't mind."

"Great, thanks. Have you reached out to Levy yet?"

"I left him a message," Raine said. "I'm sure he'll return my call soon. I know he's anxious to talk to you and Dominic."

"Yeah, well, I wish I could be sure he's on our side." She walked into the garage behind Dominic. The space was empty, so she dug her keys from her pocket. Best to keep the SUV in the garage from this point forward.

"There are no rumblings about him being untrustworthy," Raine assured her. "My boss assured me Levy is a great marshal."

"Okay. We'll be here at Grady's. See you later." She ended the call as Dom opened the connecting door to the house. She didn't follow him in, which had Smoky standing between them, as if not sure which way to go. "Go on, girl. Go with Dom."

He glanced back at her. "What are you doing?"

"Parking the SUV in the garage." She stepped closer, handing him the backpack. "Go ahead and get your computer online. We'll work until my family gets here."

"I'll need the internet password." Dom took the backpack. "I could try hacking in, but it will be quicker if your brother happens to know it."

"I'll get it for you." She wasn't surprised Dom knew how to hack into various systems. Was it possible the gunman has connections with a hacker too? Was that how they kept getting found, despite their efforts to stay off the grid?

She parked the SUV in the garage, closed the door, and joined Dominic. Smoky had stretched out between Dom and the garage door, waiting for Kendra to come in. She pulled out her phone and made another call.

This time her brother Justin answered. "Let me guess, you need the Wi-Fi password."

"If you know it." She grinned. Just knowing her brother was on the way made her feel calmer. "Otherwise, Dom can hack in."

"He can do that?" Justin sounded surprised. "Okay, the password is WingSong876."

She repeated it for Dom, who typed it in. He sent her a thumbs-up and went to work.

"Griff is on his way too," Justin informed her. "Chase wanted to come along, but Wynona has a doctor's appointment in a few hours. She has been having some false labor, so she asked Chase to accompany her, just in case."

"I hope she's okay." Kendra frowned, thinking about how Bailey had just delivered her daughter several weeks early. Naomi was still in the hospital, but her condition was stable. Trevor and Bailey were hoping to bring their daughter home soon. "We already have one premature baby in the family, we don't need another one."

"Exactly why Chase is taking Wynona to the doctor," Justin agreed. "I assured him that Griff, Raine, and I can handle things. We'll be there as quickly as possible."

"No problem. We're safe at Grady's." She couldn't imagine a better place to stay.

"See you soon." Justin ended the call.

Kendra pocketed her phone, then joined Dom at the table. He was so intent on his task he didn't seem to notice her. Remembering how he liked to drink coffee while working, she snooped in Grady's pantry. Finding coffee and filters, she quickly made a pot.

When the coffee was finished, she filled two

mugs and carried them to the table. Setting one next to Dominic, he finally looked up at her.

"Thanks."

"What can I do?" Kendra didn't like feeling helpless. "Is there some angle I can investigate?"

"I don't think so." His gaze went back to the screen. "I'm still working on the rerouting process. Once I have our connection secure, we can start looking into the three men who may have hired Stuart in Jackson Hole."

"Okay." She dropped down beside him. Their plan was still a long shot, but they had nothing better to do while they waited for Justin, Raine, and Griff to arrive.

It was a solid ten minutes before Dom glanced at her. "If this doesn't work, I'm not sure what will."

"I'm sure it's fine." She touched his arm. "You're the expert. I can't imagine any other computer geeks are smarter than you."

"Not sure about that." He grimaced. "This technique I'm using isn't necessarily new."

She squeezed his arm. "You've got this."

He nodded, then cracked his knuckles. "Let's start with the forty-nine-year-old Lamar Mortenson." Dom's fingers danced along the keyboard as he spoke. "I know we shouldn't use age as a marker, but it seems logical this guy would have been older than twenty-nine when he hired Ramsey to kill my father."

"Agree." She knew bad guys came in all shapes and sizes. Not to mention, gender. But in this case, it was logical to think a man had ordered the hit. She leaned in to see Dom's screen. "You're checking to see if he has a criminal background?"

"Yep." He frowned at the screen. "He's clean. Not even a minor arrest on his record."

"Try the next one. What was his name? Ian Bartly?"

"Bartoli," he corrected. "Ian Bartoli."

A couple of hits popped up on the screen. "Drug possession from nine years ago." She did the math. "That means he was arrested for having drugs when he was fifty-one. Seems old to have been popped for drug possession."

"Yeah, but it looks like he paid a fine and that was it." Dom sat back in his chair, his gaze focused on the screen. "A lot of rich and famous people do drugs. Maybe he's one of those that like to party hard."

"Maybe. But his arrest was in Jackson." Was that significant? She couldn't see how. "I wonder if he likes to ski. Jackson is a known ski destination for those with money."

"The arrest was in February, so that's a safe assumption." He drummed his fingers on the table.

"Not sure that's enough to consider him capable of murder."

"Maybe Raine and Griff can find a connection between Bartoli and Gunther Volter. Or Theo Le Ruiz." It felt a bit like grasping at straws. "Or we could be on the wrong path. These guys may be innocent."

"Too bad there's not an easy way to find out if any of these guys have been to South Africa." Dom sighed, then leaned forward. "I guess we should try the third guy, Timothy Platt, even if he is young."

As it turned out, the only thing that popped for Timothy Platt was a DUI from back when he was seventeen. As a lot of kids were caught drinking and driving while underage, she didn't think that moved him into a prime suspect category either.

Looking into these guys wasn't working. She rose and paced the room. Their attempts to investigate this case were laughable. They weren't cops and didn't have access to any real criminal databases. They couldn't even see if these guys had passports, much less had traveled to South Africa.

Other than the one lead Dominic had stumbled upon with Bartoli having a record for drug possession, they really had no idea who had ordered the sabotage. "We need something more. We may as well wait for Raine and Griff to get here. They'll have a better idea of where to go from here."

Dom shrugged and continued to work at the computer. As she wandered through Grady's home, Smoky stood and followed.

"Don't mind me, girl," she told the dog. "I just can't seem to sit still."

Smoky tilted her head and continued following Kendra. She felt a little guilty over not walking Smoky or spending time training with her. The K9 was highly energetic and normally enjoyed running around the ranch. Kendra vowed to make it up to Smoky once the danger was over.

Time moved slowly. So much so that she tapped her watch, worried that it had stopped working. It hadn't.

When her phone rang, she eagerly grabbed the device. "Hello?"

"Kendra, it's Raine. I heard you went to Grady's house?"

"Yes, we're digging into a couple of possible suspects." That sounded better than admitting she was pacing the room. "Where are you?"

"Still on the road. The reason I'm calling is because I just spoke to Andrew Levy. He's in Cody."

She froze, glancing at Dominic. "Why is Andrew Levy here in Cody? We never told him where we were staying."

"I'm not sure, but I don't think we can put off meeting him for much longer." Raine sounded apologetic. "We're only ten minutes away. I'll call Levy now and let him know he can meet with us at Grady's."

She tightened her grip on the phone, struck by a wave of apprehension. "Okay, if you think it's safe, then go ahead and set up the meeting. I'll feel better knowing you, Justin, and Griff will be here with us."

"Me too. Don't worry. He's not going to try anything." Raine paused, then said, "We'll be there soon. I'll ask Andrew to meet us in fifteen minutes or so. That way we'll make sure we can be there before he arrives."

"Great." Her tone lacked enthusiasm. "Thanks, Raine. See you soon."

As she lowered the phone, Dom stood. "Levy is coming here?"

"Yes. But we won't meet him alone." She crossed over to the backpack to retrieve the gun she'd stored inside while they were eating breakfast. "We're armed too."

"I don't trust him." Dom scowled and began to pace as well. "He must have tracked our new cell number. And that means he could have found us at the cabin."

Her worry morphed into full-blown fear. She quickly called Raine back. Her sister-in-law didn't answer.

Was she already on the phone with Levy? If so, they didn't have much time. "Let's get out of here."

"Really?" Dom abruptly stopped to look at her. "I thought you agreed to meeting with him here?"

"I changed my mind." Kendra couldn't explain the sudden wave of apprehension. "Let's go. We can call Raine on the way to a new location." Where, she wasn't sure. Maybe another café.

She didn't like the connection between Levy being here in Cody like the gunman. The more she thought about it, the more she believed meeting Levy in a public place was a better idea. "It's time to get out of here."

"Right behind you." Dom closed the laptop, unplugged it, and tucked it under his arm.

She grabbed her coat and shrugged it on. "Come, Smoky."

Out in the garage, she opened the back hatch for her K9. Once Smoky was settled inside with the backpack, she closed the hatch and opened the garage door. She started the car as Dominic stayed behind to close the garage door behind them.

The sky was light now. She drove out of the garage, then waited for Dominic to punch in the code. He swiftly came over to fold himself into the front seat.

She drove from Grady's house, feeling relieved when they managed to get two blocks. She pulled over to the side of the road to call Raine when she noticed a car approaching from the opposite direction. There wasn't time to duck out of sight.

It didn't matter, though, when the truck passed them without slowing down. But as the vehicle went by, she realized it was a large dark-gray truck.

The gunman? Levy? Were they one and the same?

Her heart thundering against her ribs, Kendra quickly hit the gas and sped away, watching her rearview mirror. As she turned at the next intersection, the sound of gunfire rang out. The occupants of the truck had opened fire on Grady's house!

9

———————

"That must be Levy back there!" Dom hadn't wanted to meet with the US Marshal, but now for sure he knew the guy was involved. If they hadn't followed Kendra's instincts to get out of there, they'd have been shot. Possibly killed.

No wonder they kept getting found!

"We shouldn't jump to conclusions." Kendra's expression was tense as she wove through the neighborhood, heading to the opposite side of the city. "While I agree it's suspicious, I don't think there was enough time between Raine contacting Levy and the truck showing up at Grady's."

"He's involved." Dom didn't for one minute believe the truck showing up so quickly was a coincidence. "Has to be."

"Maybe." Kendra's brow furrowed as she continued putting distance between them and Grady's home. She dug her phone from her pocket and tossed it into his lap. "The last number is Raine. Let her know what's happening."

He found the number and did as she asked. This time, the call was picked up. "Kendra?"

"It's Dom. The gunman showed up at Grady's place. We're on the road."

"What?" Raine sounded horrified. "How did that happen?"

"You tell us." Dom's tone was hard and flat. He was tired of playing nice. "Come on, Raine. The answer is obvious. Levy is a part of this. He must have been closer to Grady's than we realized to show up so fast after you made the call."

"I didn't even talk to him," Raine protested. "I mean, I did, but when I called the second time to give him Grady's address, he didn't answer."

"That's because he was here, shooting at Grady's house!" His temper flared hot. "The truck passed us seconds after we left the place. I'm telling you, he's the gunman."

"I understand your concern. It does seem odd that the gunman got there so quickly. Wait a minute, this is Levy now, calling me back." Raine paused, then added, "I'm going to take this. I'll call you back when I'm finished."

"You do that." He stabbed the end call button and slid the phone into the center console. "Raine still believes in Levy."

Kendra glanced at him. "What exactly did she say?"

"She said she never gave Levy the address because he didn't answer her call." He twisted in his seat to look behind them. There were other cars on the road now as Cody residents headed off to work. He felt naked and vulnerable driving around like this. Maybe if the SUV was made of bulletproof windows, he'd feel better. "I'm not sure that matters. Not if Levy has been tracking us all this time."

"I agree. If Levy can track our disposable phones, then he wouldn't need the address from Raine." She shook her head. "I don't like this, Dom. Not one bit."

"I know." His heart was still racing in his chest. This running from bad guys was getting old. "The good news is that we're safe now."

"Yeah." Kendra's expression was still troubled. "But that was a close call."

No lie, he thought wearily. "Where to?"

"I think we need to find another restaurant." Kendra pursed her lips. "We need a place we can meet with Raine, Justin, and Griff."

"Without Levy." He glanced at the phone in the

console. "We should probably make one last call to Raine and then ditch our new phones."

"Yeah, let's do that." Kendra shot him a quick look. "I don't want to use the Hitching Post or the Sunny Side Up Café."

He nodded. Scanning the road, he noticed a restaurant up ahead. "What about that place? Dinah's Diner."

Kendra drove past the place. "Looks only half full, which means we should be able to get a table for five."

"I'll let Raine know the plan." He reached for Kendra's phone. "Then we need to find a place far away from the diner to get rid of our phones."

"I know." Kenda's expression was solemn. "I just can't believe Levy is a part of this."

Raine answered on the first ring. "Dom? Where are you?"

He trusted Kendra's family and quickly gave her the information. "We'd like to meet with you, Justin, and Griff at Dinah's Diner, without Levy. Do you know where it is?"

"I don't, but I'm sure Justin does. We'll meet you there, and I won't let Levy know."

"Don't let him track your phone either." He knew he sounded paranoid, but he couldn't help it. "I believe he's been tracking our disposable phones. We're getting rid of them before the meeting."

"I understand. I'll toss mine too." Raine's somber voice soothed his fears. He was grateful she was taking his concerns seriously. "We'll see you soon."

"Okay." He lowered the phone, then pulled his out too. "Let me know when you find a good place to ditch these."

"I'm heading to the other side of town." She sighed. "The side that's closer to Grady's house. I figured that's best as it was our last-known location. I hope the gunman didn't damage the place too badly."

"I'm just glad we got out of there in time to avoid the attack." He understood she was concerned about her brother's friend's place. He didn't like knowing the house they'd used for what, barely forty-five minutes, had been targeted too.

Dom waited until he recognized some of the landmarks, then lowered his passenger-side window. After tossing the devices out, he lifted the window. "Okay, that's done. We can turn around now to head back."

She nodded without responding, her gaze focused on the road before them. He reached over to touch her arm. "Thank you for helping me. I know you didn't have to stay, especially with the shooter finding us at every turn."

"Yes, I did." She shot him an exasperated glance. "This involves both of us, Dom. And I really believe the best way to get this guy is to stick together."

She was amazing. Far too sweet and noble considering the nonstop danger. Dom dropped his hand and turned to look behind them. In the crate area, Smoky lifted her head.

He was struck by a wave of anger. There was no reason for anyone to kill Kendra or her K9. Him either, for that matter, but they were the true innocents in this.

Helen Gingrass had been innocent too. Her only crime was comforting a dying Stuart, listening to his confession. Now she was dead. Like his father and Kendra's parents.

No more, he silently vowed. No more death or close calls. They needed to figure out a way to trap Levy into revealing himself.

How, he had no clue. But that was something Raine and Griff could do. Or so he hoped.

Kendra continued taking side streets to make their way back to the diner. He noticed two SUVs parked side by side with back crate areas. Her family must already be inside.

After pulling into a parking spot that was two down from the other SUVs, Kendra killed the engine and opened the back hatch. "Let's head inside."

With Smoky trotting at her heels, Kendra strode toward the door. Dom fell in a step behind her, casting a glance around the area to make sure the GMC Sierra truck wasn't nearby.

The warmth of the restaurant surrounded them, along with the welcoming scent of freshly brewed coffee. Kendra wove through the restaurant to a large round table set for five. Three people were already there, although they all stood as he and Kendra approached.

One guy had Kendra's dark hair. He stood beside a petite woman who Dom assumed was his wife, Raine. The other guy had blond hair, not unlike his own.

"Hey." Kendra's smile didn't quite reach her eyes. "This is Dominic Lakeland. Dom, this is my brother Justin, his wife, Raine, and my brother-in-law Griff."

"Nice to meet you." Dom offered his hand. All three shook it, then dropped back into their seats. Smoky crawled beneath the table to join a beautiful yellow lab. If Dom hadn't noticed the thumping tail, he'd never have known there was a dog lying under there.

"I'm not sure it's really nice to meet you," Justin drawled. "Seems to me you dragged our baby sister into the line of fire."

"Knock it off, Justin. This isn't Dom's fault." Kendra narrowed her eyes. "We were working on trying to figure out what happened to our parents when the gunman found him. He's an innocent victim too."

"Kendra is right." Raine's mouth curved into a rueful smile. "Dominic didn't ask to be placed in WITSEC. That was his father's doing."

Dom didn't blame Justin for feeling protective of his sister. He held Justin's gaze. "I tried to convince Kendra to head back to the ranch. Unfortunately, it's too late now. Levy will likely try to eliminate her, too, the way he has gotten rid of the hospice nurse, Helen Gingrass."

"We don't know for sure Levy is responsible," Raine protested.

"Who else has the resources to track our disposable phones?" Dom stopped speaking as their server approached.

"Coffee?" She held up the pot. When he nodded, she poured some for him and Kendra. "Are you ready to place your order?"

"I'll stick with coffee," Dom said. He glanced at the others. "You should eat, though."

"We will." Justin rattled off his order. Raine and Griff followed suit. Kendra shook her head.

"Coffee is fine for me." She managed a smile. "Thanks."

When they were alone again, Dom leaned forward. "I'm good with technology. I was able to hide our ISP address so we could use our laptop. Yet somehow, we kept getting found."

Griff nodded. "I can see why you suspect Levy. It's possible he's involved. But why would he come after you now?"

"Because Stuart Ramsey confessed to murdering my father." Dom shrugged. "That seems to have been the inciting incident. Prior to that, I didn't have any clue that my father was in witness protection."

"That makes sense," Raine agreed. "You instigated the call to the marshal's office."

"I did." Dom frowned as he thought back. "Although I ditched my personal phone before we even got to the hotel. I used a disposable phone to call Levy. I'm not entirely sure how he figured out which disposable phones we were using. We paid for them in cash."

"Speaking of which, I have new devices for you." Justin rummaged in a backpack that looked identical to the one Kendra carried. "Here. These are from a previous operation. Also purchased with cash."

"Thanks." He took one phone, sliding the other toward Kendra. "Now we just need to figure out how to set a trap for Levy."

Raine arched a brow and glanced at Griff. Nobody spoke for a long moment. Finally, Justin said,

"He has a point. We should try to prove beyond a reasonable doubt that Levy is guilty."

"Or innocent," Raine said on a sigh.

Dom sat back in his seat, feeling satisfied that they'd agreed to his plan.

How they operationalized his idea, he thought grimly, *was up to them.*

KENDRA WISHED Justin would tone down the big brother act. Although she had to admit, Dom handled it well. Still, it was annoying to be treated like fragile glass.

"We should set up another safe house," Griff suggested. "We'll give Levy the location and be waiting for him when he shows."

"And if he's not involved?" Raine asked. "We can't just shoot first and explain our suspicions later."

"We can hide along the perimeter," Griff said. "We won't shoot first, but if he opens fire, all bets are off."

"I like it," Justin agreed.

Kendra glanced at Dom. "You're being awfully quiet."

"This isn't my area of expertise." He shrugged, then added, "But I like the idea of using a safe house. The only issue is that I'd rather not obtain that using the Sullivan name."

"We can try using Owen's last name of Ross." Kendra glanced at Griff. "I don't think Levy knows Owen is pretty much a part of the family now."

"That may work. Owen's wife, Emily, had a different last name from Doug even before she and Owen were married, which helps. Good idea, Kendra." Griff picked up his phone. "I'll let Owen know what we're up to."

Dom shot her an admiring glance. "We should have tried that ourselves."

"I didn't honestly think about it until now." She grimaced, rubbing her temple. The excess caffeine was getting to her. "Chalk it up to not having time to think clearly. Let's just hope Levy didn't do his homework, or he may suspect a trap."

"It's possible he'll play along," Justin pointed out.

"He hasn't so far," Dom argued. "We barely left Grady's house before he showed up guns blazing."

"And you're sure there isn't another way someone could have found you?" Raine glanced between Kendra and Dom. "We need to be open to all possibilities."

Kendra gestured to Dom. "Dom did a fancy technique to hide our ISP location. I don't see how the average gunman would be able to figure that out."

"Who said the gunman is average?" Griff shot back. "For all we know, he's got a computer whiz on the payroll."

"We considered that possibility," Dom admitted. "I'm not bragging, but my skills are better than most."

There was a long pause as her brother and in-laws digested that. Finally, Griff nodded. "Okay, we'll move forward on the basis it's Levy who's managed to track your disposable cell phones. We'll obtain a rental property under Owen's name, then contact Levy with the address." He gestured to the server carrying a large tray toward them. "After we eat."

The topic turned more mundane as Justin, Raine, and Griff ate. Kendra had been making plans for a Christmas gathering, but she wasn't in the mood to discuss the holidays.

The moment they finished eating, Justin pulled cash from his wallet for the tab while Griff worked his phone.

"Owen is fine with us setting up a rental in his name," Griff announced. "I found a place on the east side of the city. That should be far enough from Grady's place for our purposes. Especially as it's situated on a large one-acre lot with the backyard butting up against the woods."

"Sounds a little like Bailey's old place," Kendra said.

"About six blocks away," Griff confirmed as he set his phone aside. "It's going to take a few minutes for the rental to go through."

Kendra hoped and prayed this would work. Once they had Levy in custody, the danger would be over.

Unless, of course, Levy refused to cooperate. The thought made her sigh. Still, having him off the streets would help.

They lingered over coffee while waiting for the rental property to go through. Griff glanced at his phone, then grinned. "We're all set."

"Let's get to the rental before we call Levy." Raine rose to her feet.

"Works for me," Justin agreed.

Dom stood, towering over her brother and Griff. Kendra gave Smoky the hand signal to come. Her K9 crawled out from underneath the table, wagging her tail at the idea of going to work.

"I should put booties and a vest on Stone." Justin bent to pat his yellow lab. "He doesn't have Smoky's fur."

"That would be best." Kendra eyed his K9. "We

don't know how long we'll have to wait outside for Levy to show up."

"I'm betting it's not long," Dom said. "He didn't waste any time earlier." He turned toward Raine. "Make sure you let him know that we're at the rental house, but you're on your way. That way, he'll assume Kendra and I will be there alone."

"I will." Raine shrugged into her coat. "If he's dirty, he'll make his move."

Kendra could tell Raine wasn't convinced of Levy's culpability. It was surprising, considering her sister-in-law's recent experience proved that with enough money involved, anyone could be corrupt.

Even those sworn to uphold the law.

She and Dom strode to her SUV. Once Smoky was settled in the back, they headed toward the east side of the city.

Overhead, the cloudy sky hinted at more snow to come. Normally, she loved snow as much as Smoky did. But now she hoped it held off for a while.

The house was dark brown in color and was set back nearly fifty yards from the road. It looked nice enough. Kendra pulled into the driveway and glanced at Dom. "Probably best to leave the car out here."

He nodded. "I just hope he doesn't shoot the tires out or something equally drastic."

"If he does, we'll grab him." She pushed out of the driver's side door, opening the hatch for Smoky.

Justin and Raine stopped on the road. Her brother opened the driver's side window. "We'll park on the next block and head to the back."

"Okay." Kendra strode over to Griff as he pulled up next. "Do you have the code?"

He nodded and rattled it off. "I'm going to park on a different street as well. We'll all come in through the sides or back of the property."

"Understood." She stepped back and watched as Griff drove away, following Justin and Raine. When they were gone, she walked up to the garage door and punched in the code.

The garage was empty, as expected. Dom followed her as she headed into the house through the attached garage door, flipping lights on along the way. While it was daytime, the overcast sky kept the interior dim enough to warrant the light.

Their plan was to have Dominic stay inside the house, while the rest of them waited outside, covering the back and the sides of the property. She didn't like exposing Dominic to danger, but he'd insisted that without someone inside, their plan may not work. After the way the gunman had found Grady's house vacant, she had to admit that was something the US Marshal might check this time around.

Dominic followed her into the open-concept kitchen and living room, setting his computer on the table. He stood and looked around. "Not bad. I hope Levy shows his face very soon. I don't want you and the others freezing to death outside."

"He will." She glanced at her watch, eyeing the time. "Raine is going to make the call in five minutes. That means I need to head out."

"Okay." Dom held her gaze. "Be safe."

"You too." Leaving Dom there alone wasn't easy. She stepped closer and quickly gave him a hug. "I'll be mad if you get hurt."

"Same goes," he murmured, surprising her by pulling her closer. He held her tight for a long second but then released his grip and stepped back. "Be careful out there."

"That's the plan. Time for me to get in position." She turned to see Smoky waiting by the door. The poor dog probably needed to get busy too. "If bullets fly, get under the table. We'll handle him from there."

"I know how to duck," Dom drawled. "Seems that's all we've been doing since this started."

Since that was true, she nodded and turned away, resisting the urge to kiss Dom. "Come, Smoky."

Kendra walked back outside through the garage, then used the code again to close the garage door.

Griff had brought the rental property up on a map application to show them the location. The house faced south, and Griff had assigned her to the northern position along the back. Raine and Justin would be stationed on the east, while Griff covered the west.

They were assuming Levy would approach from the road, which made sense. Yet remembering the shadow that had inched along the woods at the cabin, Kendra knew she needed to be prepared for anything.

The good news was that Smoky would let her know with a low growl if someone approached. Levy wouldn't anticipate there would be anyone waiting outside.

Kendra jumped over the snowbank on the side of the house closest to the garage to hide her footprints, sticking close to the side of the house as she made her way to the backyard. If Levy noticed the footprints in the snow leading around to the back, he might get suspicious.

Or maybe he'd assume she was taking her dog out. Which was something she would do upon arriving to a new location. When she reached the corner overlooking the backyard, she paused and scanned the area.

The snow was undisturbed. Maybe nobody had rented the place since the most recent snowstorms.

She stayed close to the house, hunching her shoulders because the wind was coming at her through the trees. She waved a hand at the yard. "Go on, girl. Get busy."

Smoky leaped through the snow as if shot out of a cannon. Her dog buried her snout in the snow, then lifted her head and ran in a circle. After a few minutes of burning off excess energy, the K9 got down to business.

Less than a minute later, another dog joined the fray. Stone romped and played next to Smoky for several minutes, until Justin called him over.

"All set?" Raine asked. "I called Levy three minutes ago. Let's get in position."

Without protest, Griff headed to the west. Justin and Raine went to the east, the side of the house that was closest to the garage.

"Come, Smoky." Her K9 bounded over, her curvy tail wagging with anticipation. Her dog along with the others on the ranch preferred to work.

Kendra wished they could play the search game. Having a scent source for the K9 to track would be easier than setting up a sting operation.

She huddled next to the house, keeping her gaze focused on the yard. Through the patio doors, light from inside shone like a beacon. She peered inside, not surprised to see Dominic sitting with the laptop, his long legs stretched out before him.

He didn't notice her watching him, but that was okay. She expected his attention to alternate between his work and the front of the house.

The wind picked up, rattling the bare branches of the trees. Again, she scanned the yard, making note of the footprints that had been left by Justin, Raine, and Griff. Along with the myriad of paw prints.

Drawing a slow deep breath, she pressed her back against the wall. At this point, all she and the others could do was to wait for Levy to show.

While praying nobody gets hurt.

10

───────

Dominic stared at the computer, his fingers resting on the keyboard as he pretended to work. After a minute, he realized that was silly. Why not work for real? Might as well see if he could find anything more about the three men who had been at the hangar in Jackson the week before his father was murdered.

And if he still couldn't find anything useful about them, he could go back in time another week to see who else may have been there. It was the only lead they had, unless they could convince Andrew Levy to talk.

In the meantime, he'd keep searching. Once again, he rerouted the ISP address to hide his work. Even though he was searching for real, it was difficult for him not to glance through the large picture window to the road out front.

Two minutes went by. Then six. Then ten.

He honestly thought Levy would have shown up by now. Dom turned and allowed himself to look outside. His body was wound tighter than a drum, so he stretched his arms over his head to loosen up. And if anyone was watching from a distance, he hoped they'd assume he was taking a break.

Not trying to see if Levy was approaching.

Seeing nothing outside, he turned his attention back to the computer. When a large truck rolled past, he almost missed it.

Levy had taken the bait. Although this time, the guy didn't open fire on the house. It seemed more likely he'd driven past to make sure Dom was there before making his move. Good. Dom continued staring at the computer screen, imagining Levy would find a place to park and approach on foot.

Come on, he silently urged. *Show your face already!*

As if hearing him, a vehicle pulled into the driveway. That was so unexpected that Dom wondered if Levy had sent his partner driving past to approach from the back of the property. The same way Justin, Raine, and Griff had come in.

The knock at the door almost made him jump

out of his skin. What were Kendra, Justin, Raine, and Griff doing? Waiting for him to attack?

Feeling foolish, Dom approached the front door. He opened it, but only a couple of inches, staring at the forty-something-year-old man standing on the front porch.

"Dominic Lakeland?" Levy held up his badge. "I'm US Marshal Andrew Levy. You're expecting me, right?"

"Freeze!" Raine's sharp tone had Levy spinning around in surprise. "Hands where I can see them!"

"What's wrong with you?" Levy didn't raise his hands, but he didn't reach for his weapon either. Probably a good thing since Griff was covering him from the other side. The marshal looked irritated and exasperated. "What is this about? You asked me to meet with you!"

"We did." Raine didn't lower her weapon. "Kendra, take Levy's gun."

Kendra holstered her own weapon before moving forward to disarm Levy. Smoky, her K9, trotted alongside her, sniffing Levy's feet with interest. The guy scowled. "You better have a good reason for taking my gun."

"How about several shooting attempts against me and Dom?" Kendra arched a brow. "Does that work?"

"And you think I'm responsible?" The incredulous expression on Levy's face appeared genuine.

"Come inside." Dom stepped back, holding the door open. "We need to talk."

"You think?" Levy's tone dripped with sarcasm. "You're all nuts to believe I could be involved in this."

"We're operating out of an abundance of caution," Raine said as she, Justin, Kendra, and Griff came inside. Smoky and Stone chased each other around the living room until Justin and Kendra called to their respective dogs.

Both K9s obediently returned to the kitchen and crawled under the table.

Levy stood off to the side, his arms crossed over his chest, his expression unamused. "I demand you return my weapon. Immediately."

"Let's talk first," Dom suggested. "Give me one good reason why we should trust you?"

"I'm a US Marshal!" Levy shouted the words. "We protect witnesses, we don't shoot at them."

"My former boss wasn't exactly an upstanding example of a US Marshal," Raine drawled. "Anyone can be sucked in by easy money."

"Not me." Levy scowled. "I don't do this for the money. I do it because I care about putting bad guys behind bars. Which is much easier to do if you can convince citizens to testify against them in exchange for a new identity."

Dom glanced at Raine and Griff. Their expressions didn't give much away. Yet he was starting to wonder if they'd gotten this wrong.

That Andrew Levy wasn't their shooter.

"Let's all have a seat," Griff suggested. "We'll return your weapon as soon as we clear up a few things."

"Starting with how long have you been in Cody?" Dom asked. "And how did you know that's where we were?"

Levy stood for a moment, then sank into one of the kitchen chairs. There were only four seats, so Justin and Griff remained standing. "I've been in touch with the Cody police department. I learned there were several shooting attempts here in town. The sergeant said he didn't know if you were around, but I figured the shooting had to be related to you, so I headed here."

"How exactly?" Dom pressed. "You drove? You flew? Where was your starting point?"

"I drove from Denver. Took me a solid nine hours because of the snow." Levy narrowed his gaze. "Do you understand how rare it is for us to lose a witness? Those who are part of the program rarely end up getting found and killed. And those who are found typically have broken the rules in some way."

"You're saying my father broke the rules?" Dom shook his head. "I don't think so."

"That's exactly what I'm saying." Levy leaned forward. "Your father learned to fly small planes prior to his being placed into WITSEC and being relocated to Montana. When your dad arrived in Billings, he worked for the power company for the first few years. Then he met the owner of the charter company. When the old man died, he passed the plane on to your father."

Dom stared at the marshal, his thoughts whirling. He had vague memories of being with a babysitter while his dad worked. He'd just assumed his father had always been a charter pilot. But if Levy was right, then his dad had given up his job to take over the charter business.

"Hard to believe Gunther's men figured out that Gary Lakeland was an alias for whatever his real name was," Kendra protested. "They knew him as an accountant, not a pilot. How would they know?"

Levy waved a hand. "Gary Lakeland's real name was Gregory Lamb. And Gregory Lamb had a pilot's license. He was also a Certified Public Accountant. Both licenses are easily found online. And when Gary Lakeland obtained a new pilot's license under his fake name, I assume someone put two and two together to come up with four."

"How?" Dom demanded.

"We often use the same initials when relocating witnesses so it's easier to become accustomed to their new name," Levy explained patiently. "Your father was a very smart man. Like brilliant. However, thinking he could go back to being a charter pilot despite being told he needed to cut ties with everything he'd done before was a massive mistake that ended up getting him killed."

Dom wanted to rant, rave, or curse. Instead, he bit his tongue. Maybe Levy was right in that his father's taking on the role of being a charter pilot after having a pilot's license in the past had gotten him killed. There was nothing he could do about that now.

The present was a much bigger concern. Obviously, he wanted to know who paid Stuart Ramsey to kill his father. But more than that, he wanted to know who was shooting at them now. And it made sense that it must go back to the same man who had hired Stuart Ramsey to sabotage his father's plane.

"Tell me more about these shooting attempts," Levy said. "Why on earth would you assume I'm involved?"

"Because we kept getting found, despite my efforts to hide our internet connections." Dom eyed Levy. "You have the resources to track our disposable phones."

"I do, yes. But I didn't do that." Levy sighed. "I

haven't taken any shots at you. I have no reason to want you dead. Any protectee death is taken very seriously by our program. Losing your father is a stain on our record."

Dom glanced at Raine and Griff. Their expressions didn't reveal their thoughts, and he couldn't help being frustrated.

"What do you think? Can we trust him?" Dom asked.

"His weapon doesn't smell like it's been fired recently." Kendra pushed the gun toward Griff. "We can search his car, see if that reveals any new information."

"I'll make some calls. We should be able to verify when Levy left Denver." Griff left the weapon on the table, choosing instead to move into the other room to use his phone.

"Fine, you do that." Levy crossed his arms over his chest again. "You'll learn I'm telling the truth."

Dominic exchanged a glance with Kendra. He knew they were both thinking the same thing. If Levy wasn't the shooter, then who was?

And more importantly, how did he keep finding them?

KENDRA WAS GROWING convinced that Levy was one of the good guys. Smart of Griff to make sure, but if Levy had been in Denver as he claimed, he couldn't have been in the large GMC Sierra truck shooting at Dominic outside the Redwood Motel in Greybull.

And that meant the real shooter was still out there, somewhere.

Kendra leaned toward believing Levy's story since Smoky hadn't alerted on his scent. Not that she had provided her K9 with a scent source, but if her dog had caught the bad guy's scent at some point during the past fifteen hours, especially that first night when she'd crossed the shooter's tracks in the snow, she felt certain Smoky would have alerted on him.

She reached over to touch Dom's arm. Their attempt to trap the shooter hadn't quite worked out the way they'd hoped. But if Levy was innocent, then meeting with him would help fill in a few blanks.

They'd already learned that Dom's father shouldn't have gotten a pilot's license in his new name. Yet she didn't blame him for wanting to do something other than working at the power company.

"I'll make some coffee," Raine announced, breaking the long silence.

"I'll do it." Dom pulled away from Kendra and

rose to his feet. His expression appeared to be carved in stone. She hoped he wasn't feeling guilty. His father's actions weren't a reflection on Dominic. Yet she could tell he was upset by Levy's comments about his father breaking the rules of witness protection, which resulted in him being murdered.

Taking her parents down with him.

"Do you have anything else to go on?" Levy asked.

"We identified a dark-colored GMC Sierra as likely belonging to the shooter," Kendra said. "No license plate, though."

"I don't drive a GMC Sierra," Levy muttered.

"Doesn't mean you didn't get a different car to show up here," she shot back. "You can't blame us for being wary."

Levy's scowl deepened, but he didn't say anything more. The silence hung heavy in the room as they waited for Griff to finish his conversation.

"Okay, I've been able to verify your vehicle left the Denver toll road last night at seven thirty in the evening." Griff returned to the kitchen table and picked up Levy's weapon, then handed it back to him, butt first. "I'm sorry, but after everything Dom and Kendra have been through, we had a right to be concerned."

"Says you," Levy groused, holstering his

weapon. "I think you allowed your paranoia to get the best of you."

"You wouldn't say that if you understood the steps Dom has taken to keep us off the bad guy's radar." Kendra didn't care if she sounded defensive. The danger had been nonstop for what felt like days, instead of hours. "Rerouting an ISP address to hide our location isn't easy. Being found despite that made us think someone within law enforcement is involved."

"Rerouting an ISP address?" Levy shook his head. "Maybe our tech could do that, but I can't. And I doubt there're many cops out there with that ability." He glanced at Dom. "That's why we hire technical computer experts like him."

Kendra had to admit, Levy made a good point. She turned to watch Dom fill a coffeepot with water. "Dom, who else knows how to do that ISP rerouting thing?"

He shrugged and started the coffee before turning to face her. "It's a skill many computer geeks would know how to perform. It's something I've done specifically to assist our clients, which include law enforcement officials. To be honest, more bad guys use it than those of us who stay on the right side of the law."

"I'm not sure your average hired gun in

Wyoming or Montana knows how to do that," Levy said. "They'd need help."

"That's true. But with enough money, anything is possible." Kendra spread her hands wide. "If someone out there did have that ability, they could be raking in big bucks to track us down."

"What about finding and tracking a disposable cell phone?" Raine asked. "Is that also something anyone with exceptional computer skills could do?"

"Maybe, but that one is harder because we paid for those phones in cash." Dom returned to the table, his expression less grim. "They'd have to know our location and then figure out a way to hack into the store video to identify us."

That seemed less likely. She sighed, feeling as if they were spinning their wheels.

"I'm having trouble understanding why anyone would pay to have us killed," Dom said. "Especially six years after my father was killed. I'm no threat to anyone." He glanced at Levy. "I thought maybe you wanted to silence me to protect your career. But if that's not it, then why me? And why now?"

"Dom has a point." Raine frowned. "Although we know the hospice nurse, Helen Gingrass, was also killed. So it could still be related to Stuart Ramsey's confession."

All this talking in circles was giving her a

headache. When the coffeepot beeped, Dom went into the kitchen to fill several mugs.

For something to do, Kendra jumped up to carry them to the table. The sour look Levy gave her indicated he hadn't entirely forgiven them for disarming him.

Too bad. Under the circumstances, they'd done what was necessary to stay safe.

"Where do we start?" Raine asked, clearly anxious to move forward on the case. "We know it's only a matter of time before the gunman shows up again."

"Maybe we should focus on who Gunther Volter may have contacted to hire Stuart Ramsey to sabotage the plane?" Griff arched a brow at Levy. "I'm sure you have some possible suspects in mind."

"I've been going through the list of his known associates," Levy admitted. "But so far, I haven't had time to dig into them."

"Do you have a list?" Dom asked. "We can start digging into them now."

Levy sighed. "My computer is in my car."

"I'll get it." Kendra jumped up and grabbed her coat. Seeing her moving toward the door, Smoky crawled out from beneath the table to join her. She glanced at Justin, who decided to tag along. It was a good excuse to get the dogs outside.

"What do you think?" Kendra asked as they waited for their dogs to get busy.

"If Griff trusts him, then I don't see a problem." Justin turned to scan the area. "Yet I also find it interesting that the shooter hasn't shown up yet."

"I was thinking the same thing." Kendra strode over to open Levy's car door. He hadn't locked it. Smoky trotted over to take a good sniff inside. Still no alert, which gave her some reassurance that the shooter hadn't been inside Levy's car recently.

Unless she was giving her K9 more credit than she should. Maybe Smoky hadn't latched onto the bad guy's scent.

Grabbing the laptop off the passenger seat, she tried to squash her suspicions. Still, she stood for a moment and opened the laptop to see what screen was up. Unfortunately, it was password protected.

"Let's go back inside." Justin grinned. "I know what you're thinking. We'll watch him log in, see what he was doing prior to his arrival."

"Sounds good to me. Come, Smoky." She closed the laptop and walked back up to the front door.

Justin, Smoky, and Stone followed her inside.

She set the laptop in front of Levy. Then stood behind him to see the screen. He glanced over his shoulder at her, then rolled his eyes as he logged in.

A list of names was up on the screen. Not the

ISP address they were using. Or even the address of the rental property.

She stepped away and shrugged out of her coat. Dom leaned forward. "I have three names of men who chartered private planes to Jackson the week before the plane was sabotaged. Can I see the list of names you have as known associates for Gunther Volter?"

"Why don't you just give me your three names?" Levy asked. "I can search the document to see if there's a match."

Dom shrugged. "Okay, the first name is Timothy Platt, age thirty-five."

Levy entered the name in the database. "Nope. He's not on the list."

"Try Lamar Mortenson, age forty-nine," Dom said.

A moment later, Levy shook his head. "Nope. He's not on the list either. I'm not sure chartering a plane a week prior to the sabotage is a good parameter to use for narrowing the suspect pool."

"It's the best we had," Kendra said.

"The last one is Ian Bartoli, age sixty-two," Dom said. "And I can go back another week; this was just a starting point.

"Wait, Bartoli? Ian Bartoli?" Levy looked shocked. "He's a known associate. Dropped off the radar after Gunther went to jail."

"Ian Bartoli must have been the one to hire Stuart Ramsey," Kendra said, feeling a wave of relief. "He's our gunman."

"If so, he's pretty nimble considering his age," Raine said with a frown. "But that's a really good lead. We can at least issue a BOLO for the guy."

"What car is registered in his name?" Justin asked. "Can we find him that way?"

"We can try." Levy was all business now as he worked the computer. "I know how to do this much as far as tracking bad guys." He glanced at Dom, then added, "Basic stuff, yes. Fancy rerouting ISP addresses, no."

His attempt at humor lightened the mood in the room. Kendra exchanged a hopeful look with Dominic. They had a name, and that was more than what they'd had prior to this meeting with Levy.

If they hadn't tried to spring a trap on the guy, they wouldn't be having this conversation now.

"I'm surprised to see he has a driver's license in the US, issued for New Jersey." Levy looked at Dom. "That's where your father lived prior to joining the program."

Dom nodded. "Makes sense that's where Bartoli lived."

"There's more." Levy turned toward Griff. "Bartoli has dual citizenship with the US and South Africa."

"You think he's part of the same organized crime cartel as Gunther Volter?" Griff asked.

"The Randover Royals," Raine added. At Levy's surprised look, she shrugged. "I was able to get access to the file. That's the name of the cartel, the leader is known as Theo Le Ruiz. Until it was disbanded after Gunther's arrest."

"That's correct." Levy tapped his screen. "Theo Le Ruiz is dead, though. He was killed a year or so after Gunther went to jail. Could be Bartoli has taken over. I don't see a vehicle registered in Bartoli's name. Our database covers the entire United States. Nothing pops under his name. He either rented the truck or he had someone else purchase the vehicle."

"If he rented it, we should be able to find him." Raine frowned. "Unless he used a fake name and ID."

"That, or Bartoli may have hired someone to rent or drive the truck." Dom drained his coffee, setting the cup aside. "Either way, it's good to have a starting point."

"Your idea of looking at recent charters going into Jackson where Ramsey worked was a good one." Levy gave Dom a nod. "Nice job. You could have a career in law enforcement if you wanted."

Kendra placed a hand on Dominic's arm. This time, he didn't shrug it off. "Thanks, but I'm running a team at my current employer now. Not sure I'm interested in a change."

"Think about it." Levy turned back to his laptop. "You know what it's like to be in danger. Why not use your skills to help others in a similar situation?"

Kendra gently squeezed Dom's arm. She didn't know much about his current job, other than it had to do with data security, but she sensed he was intrigued by the idea of working law enforcement.

"I'll consider that. Does this mean we're working together on this moving forward?" Dom arched a brow. "Because the sooner we get this guy, the sooner Kendra and I can go back to our normal lives. She's the true innocent in all of this. The only reason she's in danger at all is because this guy targeted me."

"We still don't know why Bartoli arranged for a gunman to go after you," Griff said with a frown. "I find it hard to understand why he'd risk being caught to finish you off. There's nothing to be gained from your death."

"Simple revenge?" Kendra asked. "From what little I know about the cartels, they like to send a brutal message to anyone who dares to testify against them. Dom's father is gone, but maybe they think Dom needs to suffer too."

"Maybe. Or it could be Bartoli believes Stuart told the nurse who hired him and that she in turn told me. There's no statute of limitations on murder." Dom shrugged. "That would explain why she was killed. Although they went to great pains to make her death look like an accident. Unlike the constant stream of gunfire we've been subjected to."

"It would make more sense to make your deaths look accidental," Levy agreed. "We didn't suspect your father's plane crash to be murder. Being shot clearly indicates murder."

There was one other possibility. Maybe the ultimate goal was to get the Krugerrand coins. Helen had one and so did Dom. Kendra was about to mention her theory, but movement from outside caught her attention.

"Down!" she yelled, and yanked Dominic down beside her, as the glass window shattered beneath an onslaught of gunfire.

11

"What in the world is going on?" Levy's voice rose in alarm.

"We were found again," Dom said hoarsely. His heart thundered with the spurt of adrenaline that came from being targeted by gunfire. He should have been used to it by now, but he wasn't. The only good thing was that this incident pretty much proved Andrew Levy wasn't their shooter. The US Marshal was down under the table with the rest of them.

Thankfully, the two K9s appeared calm. Far more than he was anyway.

"We need to head out the back," Griff ordered. "Hurry!"

Dom grabbed the laptop, wondering again how they were found. He had rerouted the ISP address just an hour or so ago. And now that he thought about it, each time they were found was shortly after he'd rerouted the ISP.

"Stick close." Kendra tugged his arm. He nodded, noticing she had her weapon in hand. So did Griff, Justin, Raine, and Levy. Dom was the only one without a gun. And for some reason, that made him feel next to useless.

"Okay." For the first time since this nightmare started, he felt safe knowing he and Kendra weren't in this alone. Staying low, Kendra quickly ran toward the back door with Smoky padding softly beside her. Griff already had the back door open, scanning the backyard for signs of a threat. When Dom and Kendra got there, Griff gave them a nod.

"Let's go." Griff led the way, with Kendra and Smoky following. Dom stayed behind Kendra as Justin, Raine, and Levy came up behind him, covering his back.

While it was nice to not be alone, he didn't like everyone else risking their lives for him. Gritting his teeth, Dom tried to make himself a smaller target, despite being the tallest person in the group.

Griff led them through the snow-covered backyard to the small wooded area to the east of the rental property. Once they were within the trees, he stopped and gestured for the rest of them to huddle closer.

"What's the plan?" Levy asked. "We need to try to grab this guy."

"Yep. We're going to split up." Griff pointed to Levy. "You and I will go on either side of the house to approach the front. Raine, Justin, Kendra, and Dom should stay back."

"Works for me." Levy didn't hesitate. Dom was impressed with the US Marshal's dedication to getting this guy. "I'll take the side closest to us. You go around the other side."

"I can come too," Raine said curtly.

Griff shook his head. "Stay here in case we need backup. Or in case another shooter comes in from this direction."

Raine didn't look thrilled but nodded. "Fine."

"Great. Let's move." Griff sprinted toward the far side of the house where the attached garage was located. Levy took the closest side, reaching the house before Griff and making his way along the side of the house toward the front.

"My SUV is in the garage," Kendra said in a low whisper. "What if we need to drive out of here?"

"Our vehicle isn't far. We'll make room." Justin glanced at his K9, Stone, who stood waiting for a command. Dom noticed Smoky stood with her head up, sniffing with interest. Had Kendra's K9 gotten a whiff of the shooter?

How much more of this could they take? The

way the shooter kept finding them, Dom feared it was only a matter of time until a bullet struck one of them.

Lifting his gaze to the sky, he opened his heart to prayer. *Please, Lord Jesus, give Griff and Levy the skill and strength they need to find and arrest this man!*

On the heels of his prayer, another crack of gunfire rang out. He flinched, then glanced at Kendra. She offered a reassuring smile, stroking her free hand over Smoky's fur.

The minutes ticked by slowly. Dom's toes were growing numb with cold when suddenly the two men came running back toward them. Both Griff's and Levy's expressions were somber.

Not good.

"What happened?" Raine demanded.

"He's gone." Levy sounded disgusted. "I fired at his vehicle as he passed by but must have missed."

"I wasn't even sure that was the right truck," Griff drawled, his gaze narrowing at Levy. "Did you get a look at the driver?"

Levy grimaced. "A brief glimpse. He's a young white guy late twenties or early thirties. But the truck was definitely a black GMC Sierra, so I figured I'd take the shot."

"A white guy in his late twenties and early thirties doesn't narrow our suspect pool," Raine said with a sigh. "What about a license plate?"

Levy frowned. "I looked but didn't see any-thing. Maybe it was covered in snow? I can't be sure."

"I didn't see a plate either," Griff admitted. "We'll call the local cops and let them know about the GMC Sierra. If they see a black one with an ob-structed plate, they have grounds to pull the driver over. Maybe our guy has a criminal record."

"Even if he doesn't, we could ask for the police to provide us his name and date of birth," Raine said thoughtfully.

"Yep," Justin agreed. "Then we can cross-check him with Bartoli."

The faint wail of sirens could be heard in the distance. Dom realized someone had called in the gunfire, alerting the police. Something he should have done once they were safely out of the house and away from the gunman.

Dom swallowed a surge of frustration. Once again, the shooter had taken shots at them without exposing himself to danger. Firing at a house from behind the wheel of a car seemed like a coward's way out. And it was also odd in that the shooter would be less likely to hit his target from that distance.

That was the point, right? To hit and kill Dom? Because he had been told too much?

"Let's get back to the house," Griff said, interrupting his thoughts. "The local police will be there soon. And we'll need another place to stay."

"We're running out of options," Kendra said dryly. "At this rate, no one will want to rent to a Sullivan."

"I'll use my FBI resources to obtain a safe house," Griff said. "Remember, we rented this specifically to draw the shooter out."

"You did?" Levy looked surprised.

Dom nodded. "Yep, that was when we suspected you were dirty. Obviously, we were wrong about that. But the other factor here is that I rerouted the ISP address to use the computer. The same way I have been each time we found a place to stay. From the hotel to one safe house and the next."

"So?" Levy lifted his hands. "I don't understand your point."

"I think we need to consider the possibility Bartoli has a hacker on the payroll." Dom held Levy's gaze, then turned to look at Kendra. "You know that it wasn't long after we got to the safe house that we didn't even rent through legal channels that we were found there. The more I think about it, the more I think there's a hacker out there feeding the gunman our location."

There was a moment of silence as the group absorbed his theory.

"Okay, we'll consider ways to narrow down who

Bartoli may have hired. How, I'm not sure. For now, we need to update the local police. Let's go." Griff turned and led the way back to the rental house. Everyone else followed. Dom fell into step beside Kendra and Smoky.

"You really think a hacker is involved?" she asked in a low voice.

"Yeah, I do." Dom grimaced as he considered for the first time that maybe someone within Data Intelligence Services could be involved. It was the largest computer technology company in the quad state area, covering Montana, Wyoming, Colorado, and Idaho.

Not that his employer was the only one who hired geeks like him for their technical expertise. The truth was that the computer industry was growing, and there were companies like Data Intelligence Services popping up all over the US and worldwide.

The dark web had tentacles that reached to every corner of the world. Their hacker could be from anywhere. Even overseas. Yet Dom didn't think so. He wasn't a cop, but in his humble opinion, digging into the employees within his company, Data Intelligence Services, would be the best place to start.

But first, they needed a safe place with internet access that wasn't likely to get them all killed.

~

KENDRA NOTICED Smoky continued to sniff their surroundings with interest. Almost as if there was something about the GMC Sierra that had caught her K9's attention. But that didn't seem possible. Despite being highly trained, even a K9 couldn't sniff through glass and steel.

The warmth of the house enveloped her when they walked inside. She sighed in relief as her fingers and toes thawed out. But then she glanced at the shattered front window that was clearly allowing cold air to seep in. The warmth wouldn't last for long, making her wish, and not for the first time, that she had a coat as warm and fluffy as Smoky's fur.

The sirens were loud enough now that they couldn't hear each other speak. Griff headed out the front door with Levy trailing behind him to meet the Cody cops.

Justin and Raine were off speaking in low voices. Kendra glanced at Dom, who set the computer on the kitchen table, then headed to the counter.

"Need more coffee," he muttered.

"What if this is about the Krugerrand coins?" Kendra spoke softly as she joined him in the kitchen. "I was going to mention this earlier, but your father obviously had some from prior to his being relocated into witness protection. Stuart Ramsey had one, either from being paid in Krugerrand or having found one when he messed with your father's plane. And then Stuart gave his to Helen, who also ended up dead."

After finishing with the coffee, Dom turned to stare at her. "I get where you're going with that thought, but keep in mind, my father doesn't have any Krugerrand at the house. I would have found it if he did. And if Bartoli thought my dad had Krugerrand on his plane, wouldn't he have taken the coins first, then killed him?"

"Maybe Stuart Ramsey found the Krugerrand on the plane just before he sabotaged the plane's engine." She warmed to her theory. "He could have told Bartoli about what he found only after your dad took off with my parents to fly back to Wyoming. Could be that Ramsey secretly kept some of the coins for himself."

"Okay, but then why come after me now? Six years later?" Dom crossed his arms over his chest, propping his lean hips against the counter. "This danger now has to be connected to Stuart Ramsey's deathbed confession."

"Yeah." Kendra nodded slowly. "I can see how that could be the catalyst here. But I still think the Krugerrand coins are significant."

Before Dom could respond, the front door

opened. Griff and Levy were accompanied by two Cody police officers, Burt Jones and Heath Anderson.

Burt eyed her grimly, then relaxed when he saw Justin and Raine standing nearby. Thanks to her older siblings, Burt Jones was overly protective of her. She had to smile when Stone and Smoky wagged their tails in greeting.

Burt bent to pet each of the dogs before addressing her. "How did this gunman find you again?"

"We're not sure." She glanced at Dom, not sure that it was worth going into detail about their hacker theory. "Did Andrew Levy tell you that he verified the vehicle was a black GMC Sierra truck? And that the license plate was covered with snow or something similar?"

"He did." Burt nodded. "We've updated the BOLO accordingly."

"Great." She stepped back when Dom approached with two cups of coffee for the two officers. "The sooner the officers patrolling the street find it, the better."

"We're doing our best." Heath sounded a little testy.

"I know you are." The last thing she wanted was to annoy the officers. The Sullivans had been through a lot over this past year, and they needed to keep their good working relationships with the local authorities. "We just thought the updated information would help."

"It will." Burt sipped his coffee, eyeing her over the rim. "You don't have anything else for us to go on, like a description of the shooter?"

"Unfortunately, nothing more than a white guy in his twenties or early thirties." Dom shrugged. "I think it's interesting that these recent attempts have been from a distance. Like he's not willing to get too close for fear we'll return fire."

"That's a good observation," Kendra agreed. "You quickly returned fire when we were at the hotel, remember? The shooter must have been caught off guard by us having a weapon, although I'm not sure why, and has decided to keep his distance moving forward."

"Great," Heath muttered. "That's only going to make it harder to find him."

"We'll find him." Burt turned to face Griff. "Where will you take Kendra and Dom next? Somewhere we can help keep an eye on them?"

"I'm working on a safe house." Griff glanced at her, then toward Justin and Raine. "I'm waiting for my boss to get back to me. In the meantime, we won't use the Sullivan name moving forward."

"Or Dom's name," she added. "He's the main target."

"Yep, we need to be incognito." Griff looked down at his phone. "This is my boss now." He swiped his finger over the screen and moved to the other side of the room where it was quieter to talk.

"I may have dinged the truck," Levy said to the second pair of officers who arrived. "I tried to disable it but must have misjudged the distance."

"Any other markings on the truck?" Sergeant Tom Howell asked. "Other than the license plate being covered with snow."

Levy stared down at the floor for a moment, then sighed. "No, I remember glancing at the driver, trying to shoot at the truck, then seeing the covered plate. I'm disappointed I missed him."

"We'll find him." Howell turned toward her. "Have you asked Smoky to find shell casings?"

"No, but we can do that now. Come, Smoky." Kendra headed into the kitchen to fill a bowl with water, setting it on the floor for her K9. Justin did the same with Stone. She grabbed her backpack so that she'd have the stuffed hippo to use as a reward.

After both dogs had lapped at the water, she turned to the door. "Let's go, Smoky!"

"Come, Stone," Justin added.

Outside, she took Smoky to one side of the house. Justin and Stone stayed on the other side to avoid both dogs alerting on the same shell casing.

She bent down and held Smoky's gaze. "Are you ready? Huh, girl? Search! Search for gold!"

Justin gave Stone the same command, and both dogs eagerly went to work. Smoky trotted along the side of the road sniffing intently. Stone moved farther down the street.

It didn't take too long. Smoky alerted first, but it was only a few seconds later that Stone did the same. Kendra approached Smoky, pulling the hippo from her bag. Seeing the shell casing in the snow, she injected praise in her tone. "Good girl! Good girl, Smoky." When she tossed the hippo into the air, her K9 leaped up to snatch it.

Soon Stone and Smoky were running around the yard with their respective rewards. She turned to see Heath Anderson beside her. "Here's one casing. Stone found one farther down."

The Cody police officer placed the shell casings into two evidence bags. He turned toward her. "What about searching the side of the house where US Marshal Levy fired his weapon?"

"I'll do that, come, Stone." Justin called his K9 over. Less than five minutes later, Stone alerted again.

"He only fired twice?" Heath asked.

Kendra pursed her lips. "I thought I heard more shots than that, three or four? But it could be that those shells landed inside the truck."

"Yeah, okay." Heath crossed over to where Stone alerted. "Thanks for your help with this."

"Anytime." Justin bent to rub his hands over Stone's fur. "Our K9s love to work, huh, boy?"

Kendra held out her palm. "Hand." Smoky trotted over and dropped the stuffed hippo into her palm. Kendra tucked it away, then turned to head back inside.

"Do you think Griff will get the feds to cough up a safe house?" Justin asked as he joined her.

"I hope so." She grimaced. "We could use a break. The danger has been relentless."

"Yeah. And I'm not sure about the hacker angle." Her brother shot her a questioning look. "Is that even possible?"

"I'm not the expert, Dom is." She tried not to sigh. The family seemed to think she knew more about computer stuff than she did. "If he thinks a hacker is involved, I believe him."

"You trust him?" Justin grabbed her arm to stop her from going inside. "I mean, you're sure he's not part of this?"

"Yes, I trust him. He's the one in danger." She kept her voice firm. "He didn't ask to go into witness protection. That was his father's doing. And that was only after the cartel murdered his mother. Dom's a good guy. He's done his best to protect me every step of the way."

"Okay, if you say so." Justin had obviously taken orders from Chase to vet Dom. "He looks like he's interested in being more than your friend and co-investigator."

"You're delusional." Kendra yanked free and opened the door, even though her foolish heart leaped in her chest at the thought of Dom being interested in her. Not that there was any chance at a future. "You're just jealous because he's taller than all of you."

"Yeah, he is, but that's not it," Justin said. "I don't want him taking advantage of you."

She almost mentioned the fact that she'd kissed him but managed to hold her tongue. Her siblings didn't need to know about her growing feelings for Dominic.

The Cody police officers cordoned off the scene, huddling together outside the rental house as they discussed their next steps.

"There you are," Griff said when she and Justin went back inside. "I have a place we can stay that is owned by the feds. No ties to you or Dominic."

"What about internet access?" Dom asked.

"There is internet access." Griff arched a brow. "But I thought you were concerned about being found by a hacker."

"I am. A hacker is the only answer that makes sense as to how we keep getting found at each location. Even those where we haven't left so much as a paper trail." Dom shrugged. "But I can think of another trick I can try to make sure to hide our electronic trail."

"I'm not sure you should do that while being held in a federal safe house," Levy protested. "Where are you going to go if that place becomes compromised?"

"I don't know, but I think we need to continue digging into Bartoli's connections." Dom glanced at her, then to Griff, Justin, and Raine. "Don't you? I mean, how else are we going to find this guy? We've identified the truck, but without plates, it's not likely to be found. And for all we know, the shooter has ditched the truck for something else."

Griff rubbed his jaw. "Yeah, I agree, we do need to keep investigating. The internet access is connected through the federal government, so I'm not sure if you'll be able to use your new trick."

Dom offered a lopsided smile. "No offense, but I'm pretty sure I can."

Griff inclined his head. "I know you're good, so no argument here. For now, let's head over to the new place. It's an isolated cabin located a few miles to the east of Cody, tucked off into the woods."

"In the woods, huh?" Justin sighed. "Good thing we have four-wheel drive."

Kendra frowned. "Okay, but help me understand

how this will work. Are you thinking we'll all follow each other there like a mini caravan? That might be a bit noticeable."

"Yes, we'll follow each other, but we'll take the back roads," Griff explained. "There's a little-known highway that winds to the north around town that will take us there. As Justin pointed out, our vehicles with four-wheel drive will come in handy."

Kendra nodded, reminding herself to have faith that Griff knew what he was doing. Her brother-in-law had never steered them wrong. Levy was one of the good guys, too, but she didn't trust him the way she trusted Griff.

With her life and Dom's.

"Works for me," Raine said. "And I agree about needing to continue our investigation. We absolutely need something more to go on to find this guy."

"I have an idea about that," Dom said. "I hate to say it, but we may want to start digging through the employees who work at Data Intelligence Services."

"What's that?" Justin asked. "A known group of hackers?"

"Not exactly. Data Intelligence Services is the company I work for. But I happen to know there are a lot of employees, guys and girls who may have done some hacking on the side." Dom grimaced. "Nothing too terrible or they wouldn't pass the background check to be hired on as employees. But if I'm being honest, I've taught a few of them how to bypass or alter the ISP address to hide access the same way I do."

Kendra frowned. "Are you saying you actually taught your coworkers how to hide their location from others?"

"Well, hiding from others wasn't really the intent, but yeah. It's a handy skill to have when you're testing data programs for weaknesses." He shrugged. "I never intended the skill to be used to break the law or anything like that. It's one of many tools we use to build secure systems."

Kendra remembered watching Dom work. "I tried to follow what you did, but it was way over my head. If you ask me, only someone with advanced skills could pull that off."

"But what Dom is saying is that a lot of people in his computer software industry can probably do that, right?" Raine asked.

"Yes," Dom said. "I taught myself, so others could do the same. As Kendra said, it's highly technical. That's why I think Bartoli may have hired a hacker."

"I'm too old for this," Levy muttered. He raked his hands through his hair. "And I don't like knowing the whole Sullivan family might be in danger now too. Maybe we need to consider a different alternative."

"Like what?" Kendra turned to face the marshal. "Are you thinking of setting another trap for this guy?"

Levy made a face. "I was thinking more along the lines of helping Dominic disappear. For good."

It took Kendra a moment to understand what Levy meant. "You mean, putting him into the witness protection program?"

"Exactly." Levy spread his hands. "Why not? If Dominic disappears, the danger is over. Everybody can go home and live their own lives."

Kendra's chest tightened to the point she couldn't draw a breath. Every muscle in her body rejected the idea of Dominic disappearing from her life, forever.

No way. There had to be another answer. Even if having a personal relationship with Dominic was out of the question, she couldn't bear the thought of him being forced to cut ties with his friends, move to a new location, and take on a new identity and a new job. Leaving everything he knew and cared about behind.

It was the bad guys who should suffer. Not Dominic. Especially since Dom hadn't done anything to deserve this.

12

"I'm not giving up my entire life." Dom glared at Levy. He hadn't liked the US Marshal before, and now it was all he could do not to slug the guy. "Besides, you can't guarantee the danger to Kendra and her family would be over. The shooter hasn't cared if he takes her out with me."

"You're the main target," Levy insisted.

"You don't know that." Dom turned, raking his hands through his hair. "Helen Gingrass was killed because Stuart confessed to her. Kendra's been with me since the beginning. If Bartoli is behind this, he'll assume that everything Stuart told Helen was passed on to me and to Kendra too." He flung his hand toward Justin, Raine, and Griff. "And that includes her extended family."

"I agree with Dominic," Justin said. "The

gunman shot through the window at the house aiming at everyone sitting around the table. It wasn't just Dom who was in danger. As far as I'm concerned, we're all in this together."

"I feel the same way," Griff added. "This thing has gotten too big to think that relocating Dominic into WITSEC will stop the danger. We need to focus on getting this guy. We think he's a hired gun, and if that's the case, then we'll convince him to turn on his boss."

"I'm in agreement with that too." Raine smiled grimly. "If anyone should be forced into WITSEC, it's the gunman. Not Dominic."

Dom was touched at how readily the Sullivan clan jumped to his defense. It occurred to him that if he hadn't met up with Kendra to work the case with her, he may have been forced to make the same decision his father had made twenty-five years ago.

Thinking about that gave him new appreciation for how difficult that must have been for his father. Becoming a widowed father to a three-year-old and having to move across the country to a start a new life without any family support.

His father had done that and more for him, Dom knew. Given up everything for the child who deserved to be protected at all costs.

If Dom had a child, he'd do the same thing. And that thought gave him pause. If the only way to keep

Kendra safe was to give up his life, the decision to enter the program would be easy. For a moment, he froze, staring blinding through the bullet-ridden glass of the living room window.

Was he being selfish? Did Levy have a point?

He abruptly turned to face the US Marshal. "Do you honestly think that if we faked my death, Kendra and her family would be safe?"

"I think it's a strong possibility, yes," Levy said.

"No, Dom." Kendra rushed over to grasp his arm. "Don't do this. I don't want you to give up everything on the slim chance the danger will be over. Besides, that's not justice for our parents. Why would you want Bartoli to get away with murder?"

He covered her hand with his. "I don't want him to get away with it. But this is my father's mess, Kendra. Not yours. Your safety is more important to me . . ."

"Hold on," Griff interrupted. "We're not going to do anything crazy. Let's get out of here and discuss further when we're at the safe house. Our first step is to come up with a plan that will draw the shooter out into the open."

"I agree," Raine said. "Convincing the shooter to turn on his employer is the best option we have. I think we need to leave, too, while the police are still hanging around outside. The shooter isn't going to come back as long as they're around. That being said, I don't think they need to know the location of the safe house. The fewer the better."

"Raine and I left our vehicle to the east a few blocks away," Justin said. "Griff, I know yours is on the other side of the neighborhood. Kendra, you and Dom should give us a few minutes to get our SUVs, then head out. We'll meet up with you to form our caravan."

"That works for me." Kendra's expression filled with relief as she released his arm. "Dom, grab the laptop. I need my backpack too."

Levy didn't look happy but gave up the argument. At least for now. As Justin, Raine, Stone, and Griff filed from the room, Levy took a step toward the front door. "I'll go first, as I need to move my car out of the driveway, behind your SUV."

Dominic crossed to the kitchen table to hand Kendra the backpack. It was heavier than he anticipated, so he slung it over his shoulder and picked up the laptop. "I'm ready."

"We're supposed to wait a few minutes for Justin, Raine, and Griff to get in position." Kendra glanced down at her K9. "But I can't just stand here either. Let's head out. I'll give Smoky time to get busy."

Dom followed her outside. Levy was already in his car backing out of the driveway. He watched as the US Marshal skirted around a Cody squad to head west. He couldn't shake the idea of going into WITSEC to keep Kendra safe.

First, her parents were innocent victims when his father was murdered. Now he'd dragged Kendra into the same danger. Granted, when they'd arranged to meet, he wasn't aware of the danger.

But he was now.

"Get busy," Kendra called to Smoky.

The Alaskan malamute did her thing, then trotted toward Kendra, her curvy tail wagging. Kendra bent to stroke the fluffy fur, then straightened to head toward the SUV parked in the driveway.

After Kendra opened the back hatch for Smoky, Dom stored her backpack and the laptop on the floor, then slid into the passenger seat.

"You're awfully quiet." Kendra sent him an arched look as she started the SUV and drove down the driveway past the police cars. "What's wrong?"

He shrugged. "I can't help but wonder if Levy is right. If Bartoli thinks I'm dead, you'd be in the clear."

"Please don't." Her pleading tone tugged at his heart. "Don't give up your entire life because Levy suggested it."

He wasn't sure how to explain to her that she was the main reason he was tempted to go along with the plan. As he stared out the passenger-side window, his heart felt heavy. Kendra was beautiful, kind, sweet, and caring.

And he was falling for her big time.

A pair of headlights flashed on and off. He pushed his complicated feelings for Kendra aside and gestured toward them. "Is that Griff?"

"I believe so." Kendra flashed her lights in response. "Yes, that's Griff. I can tell by his license plate."

"You know your siblings license plate numbers?"

"Yeah. I know it sounds weird, but Chase made us memorize them. Along with our phone numbers." She lifted a shoulder. "It's come in handy over this past year, as my siblings have gotten themselves in some dicey situations." She grinned. "Like now."

He'd wondered why the Sullivans seemed so calm and cool in a crisis. He'd thought it was probably their search and rescue training, but it was more than that.

"That's Griff, and I think Levy is behind us." Kendra's gaze bounced from the rearview mirror to the side mirrors. "I don't see Justin and Raine, but if they were to the east, they'll end up behind Levy."

"I'm not sure I like the caravan approach." He twisted in his seat to look through the back window. Smoky was stretched out in the crate area, resting with her eyes closed. "I feel like we're waving a neon sign that says 'Follow us!'"

"The shooter isn't going to hang around nearby with the police swarming around outside." She reached over to pat his knee. "I have faith that Griff and Raine know what they're doing."

"Of course they do. It's just so different from how we tried so hard to fly under the radar." Drawing in a deep breath, he tried to relax. Her hand was warm on his knee that was painfully jammed up against the dashboard. He reached over to grasp her fingers. "Kendra, I need you to promise me you'll be careful. I'll feel guilty if you get hurt."

"Guilty?" She frowned and tightened her grip on his. "I made the choice to come and to stay with you. There's absolutely nothing for you to feel guilty about. I don't even want to think about what might have happened if you'd stayed in Billings."

He wondered about that for a moment. What if he had stayed in Billings? The snowstorm had made him consider canceling, but he'd decided to push forward. The first attack against him hadn't come until he'd arrived at the Redwood Motel. Was that because someone had shown up at his place only to realize he was gone? But if that was the case, how did the gunman know to find him at the Redwood Motel?

Something nebulous niggled at the back of his mind. He couldn't seem to put his finger on what was bothering him. Dom hoped he wasn't missing something important.

"Don't forget, we have God on our side," Kendra said softly.

"I know." He was starting to believe she was right about that. It certainly seemed as if they managed to escape danger every time the shooter showed up.

Dom stared at the overcast sky and silently prayed that God would guide him to making the right decision when it came to protecting Kendra. Somehow, she had become the most important person in his life.

He would risk his life for hers without hesitation.

SENSING DOMINIC'S TENSION, Kendra tried to think of a way to convince him not to go into witness protection. Of course, if that was the best option to ensure his safety, then she would absolutely encourage him to go that route. Even if that meant losing him. Yet she didn't want him making a drastic move because Levy seemed to think she would no longer be in danger. His theory didn't ring true in her opinion. Not after she'd been glued to Dom's side for the past thirty-six hours.

"We'll work this out together," she said, after a long silence. "I know I'm not as helpful with computer stuff, but Griff and Raine will help dive into Bartoli's connections. And if there's a way to trap the gunman into making a move, that will blow this thing wide open."

"I hope you're right." Dom surprised her by pressing a quick kiss to the back of her hand. "Bad enough my father ended up taking two innocent people down with him. I refuse to make the same mistake."

"That wasn't your father's decision." She frowned at him. "Your father was a victim in this too. Just like my parents."

Dom shrugged and released her hand. "How much farther until we reach the safe house?"

"Griff is turning left at the next intersection." She waved toward the lead SUV with its blinker on. "Looks like the road isn't as well plowed as the others."

"Yeah." Dom shifted in his seat. "If you need me to drive . . ."

"I'm fine." She gripped the steering wheel tight as she made the turn. The wheels chugged through the snow without a problem. "I'm sorry the SUV is smaller than what you're used to."

"I'll survive." He didn't look at her, keeping his

gaze on the road. "There doesn't seem to be much traffic."

"That's a good thing. Hopefully, the shooter is far away and will have no way to track us moving forward." She pushed her SUV forward, following Griff's taillights. There weren't a lot of residential homes either, which was why there wasn't a lot of traffic. She wasn't as familiar with this part of the city.

There were deeper drifts of snow in the open areas from the wind. Kendra kept her pace steady, fearing if she slowed down, she'd get stuck.

After what seemed like a lifetime, Griff took another turn. This highway had been plowed recently.

Another fifteen minutes passed before Griff tapped his brakes. Kendra leaned forward, trying to see beyond Griff's SUV. When he turned to the left, she belatedly realized he'd reached the driveway.

She hit the gas, forcing her car through the deep snow. Following Griff's tire tracks helped and soon she could see a large log cabin flanked by tall evergreen trees.

"Wow, this looks really nice," she said as she came to a stop beside Griff. Her brother-in-law was out of his car and walking up to the front door. She assumed he had a key code, much like those used by rental properties.

"Yeah." Dom scowled as he pushed open his

passenger-side door. "I hope this doesn't get shot up like the last place."

She flashed him an annoyed look. "Come on, Dom. This is a federal safe house. Let's stay positive, okay? No more doom and gloom."

He shrugged and shifted to get out. She hit the back hatch, freeing Smoky. Dom grabbed her backpack and the laptop. She crossed to the back of the SUV to close the door. "Come, Smoky."

She and Dominic headed up to the log cabin. A moment later, Levy, Raine, Justin, and Stone pulled up behind them.

Smoky wheeled and took off after Stone. She sighed and slipped around Dominic to get control of her K9. She understood her high-energy dog hadn't had much play/work time, but Smoky needed to obey her commands.

"Smoky, come!" Her sharp voice told the K9 she wasn't messing around.

Thankfully, Smoky stopped abruptly and turned, running to her side. She gave Smoky the hand signal to heel, and the dog sat, staring up at her adoringly.

"Good girl." She stroked Smoky's fur. "Good girl."

Justin and Stone joined her as they headed up to the house. Dom stood in the doorway, watching as if he were afraid the shooter might show up at any moment. Justin nodded toward him. "He's really worried about you."

"For some reason, he feels guilty about this." She frowned. "As if it's his fault Stuart Ramsey confessed to killing his father."

"Yeah, I agree he's an innocent victim in this." Justin shot her a sidelong glance. "And if he feels guilty, it's because he's worried about you, Kendra."

She hoped her brother couldn't see her blush. "He's a good person, he'd care about anyone being in danger."

"Yeah, you keep telling yourself that, sis." Justin patted her on the back. "He's crushing on you."

Highly doubtful that Dom was crushing on her, but she decided there was no point in arguing with Justin. Her older brothers liked to stick their nose into her personal business. Further denials would only make Justin think she was crushing on Dom too.

Maybe she was, but that was something she had no intention of confiding to Justin. Even if she was closest to him compared to the others.

Her brother opened the front door for her. A wave of warmth washed over her from the blazing fire in the great room. Smoky and Stone ran around the living room for a moment, until Justin directed them to sit under the table. Kendra eyed the massive stone fireplace that extended all the way up the cathedral ceiling. A curved staircase led to the second-floor bedrooms, and the hallway loft overlooked the living and kitchen area.

She had no idea how many bedrooms were up there, but this was by far the nicest place she'd ever stayed.

"You feds get paid too much if this is your safe house," Levy drawled, looking around with his hands on his hips. "We don't get this level of treatment. Then again, most of our witnesses are scumbags."

"Not my father," Dom quickly interjected.

"Whoa, I said most, not all." Levy looked embarrassed at being called out.

"Okay, let's talk about how we can draw the shooter out so that we can grab him." Griff took over the conversation. Kendra could tell her brother-in-law wasn't thrilled about Levy's comments either. She imagined Levy had worked with a lot of bad guys, which had likely grated on him after a while. Still, he shouldn't paint every witness with the same blackened brush.

"I think we need to focus on Bartoli's known contacts." Raine reached down to stroke Stone's soft fur beneath the table. "He's high on our suspect list. We can also try to see if any of the employees at Dom's company are involved."

Kendra glanced at Dom. "Are you sure about your new trick to reroute the ISP address?"

He shrugged. "Nothing is one hundred percent."

"Okay, that's a starting point." Justin moved into the kitchen. "I don't suppose we have anything to eat here?"

"Check the freezer," Griff suggested. "Frozen pizza is better than nothing."

Kendra didn't feel very hungry, but the hour was going on noon. They'd spent more time at the last rental property than she'd anticipated. "We should have stopped to grab something along the way."

"Levy, maybe you can head back to pick up lunch?" Raine gestured to the driveway. "You have a clear pathway out of here."

Levy frowned, then shrugged. "Sure, if that's what you want."

"No need, there are three frozen pizzas in the freezer," Justin said. "I'll toss these into the oven now and figure out something else for dinner."

As Justin went to work on their frozen pizzas, Dominic set the laptop on the kitchen table and turned it on. "Give me a few minutes to see if I can get into the network the feds have here."

"I still think placing Dominic in witness protection is the way to go," Levy groused. "We shouldn't have lost his father to a plane crash. I don't want to be known as the US Marshal who also let his son be killed."

"No." Kendra's tone was sharp. "Drop it. We're going to work on a way to arrest the shooter. Then you and Griff will convince him to turn on his employer."

"You're assuming the shooter knows Bartoli's real name," Levey pointed out. "Bartoli is smart enough to use a middleman to make the deal."

"Fine, then we'll get that guy's name and convince him to cooperate." She drilled Levy with a hard look. "Those are the types of people who end up in witness protection, right? That's what you just said."

"Fine." Levy dropped into the closest chair and crossed his arms over his chest. "You guys take the lead on this. I'll help in any way I can."

She didn't appreciate Levy's hands-off approach, feeling as if he was just waiting for the opportunity to say, *I told you so*. Then again, she could maybe understand that he was worried about his reputation, especially if he lost another witness.

Her only concern was to find and arrest Bartoli so he could be held accountable for murdering Dom's father and her parents. That was the only way to ensure that she and Dominic would be safe.

A few minutes passed while Dominic worked at the computer. But then he abruptly stopped, sat back in his chair, and pressed the palms of his hands against his eyes. "I changed my mind. You need to set me up as bait." He dropped his hands and looked between Griff and Levy. "Rent another safe house and put me in plain sight. I'll log into the internet and draw the shooter out into the open. That worked before when we thought Levy was the bad guy."

"No way," Levy protested. "It's not smart for you to be there alone. At the very least, I need to be with you."

"Yeah, I don't like that idea either." Griff gestured to the laptop. "What's wrong, can't you bypass the internet the way you'd hoped?"

"No, I can do it," Dom said. "But I'm not sure I should. I just can't shake the fact that every single time I bypass the ISP address, we get found. It's almost like that move alone is drawing attention to our location."

"Is that possible?" Kendra asked. "I mean, does what you're doing leave enough of an electronic footprint to make it obvious where we are?"

"No, it shouldn't." Dom sighed loudly. "But I'm second-guessing myself now that I'm about to do it again. We're pretty much out in the middle of nowhere. If this guy shows up, it will take longer for the police to get here."

"Yeah, but this time, the shooter would have to

get closer to the house to try taking you out," Raine said. "Maybe this is the best place to use to draw him out."

"Maybe he'll bring reinforcements this time," Dom said. "If you're right about Bartoli using a middleman to take me out, they must be getting nervous that the job hasn't been completed yet. How much longer before he gets antsy and sends more gunmen after us?"

The thought of a small army coming after them made Kendra's blood run cold.

"Let's decide this after we eat," Justin said from the kitchen. "The pizzas will be ready in less than ten minutes."

"Yeah, it's probably better to avoid going on the run without food in our systems," Griff said, half joking, half serious. "I'm starving."

"Fine." Dom closed the laptop. "I won't do anything yet."

Kendra pulled another chair over from the living room so they could all eat at the table. When the pizza was finished, Justin cut them up and piled the slices on a large platter.

"We need to say grace," Raine said, as Levy moved to grab a slice.

Kendra had to smile at the surprised look on Levy's features. But the US Marshal folded his hands in his lap and bowed his head.

Griff cleared his throat. "Dear Lord Jesus, we ask You to keep us all safe in Your care. Please bless this food and give us the strength and courage to find those who would do us harm. Amen."

"Amen," Kendra, Dom, Justin, and Raine repeated. Levy bobbed his head without answering.

The dogs shifted beneath the table, no doubt getting restless. When they finished eating, Raine jumped to her feet and carried empty plates to the kitchen. Kendra chipped in to help with clean-up duty, then noticed Smoky had moved toward the front door, looking at her expectantly.

"Okay, girl. I'm coming." She reached for her coat, then glanced back at Dom. "Don't make any decisions until I get back."

He nodded. "Understood."

Kendra shoved her feet into her boots, opened the front door, and held it open for Smoky. Her Alaskan malamute ran outside as if desperate to get busy. Kendra followed her K9 as the dog headed out toward the side of the house where one of the large evergreen trees was located. Smoky didn't pee on trees the way the male dogs did, but she sniffed the area around the tree with interest.

"Come on, girl. Get busy." Kendra hunched her shoulders against the cold wind coming from the north. There was a low rumbling sound in the distance that made her wonder if someone was driving down the road. She turned to look for headlights or the dark shape of a car but didn't see anything.

Smoky did her thing but then turned and sniffed the breeze. Suddenly the dog turned and ran around the pine tree as if she'd caught an interesting scent.

"Smoky!" Kendra broke into a run, fearing her K9 had latched on to the scent of a moose or an elk. Especially as Smoky was heading in the opposite direction from the road. As she rounded the tree, she heard a sharp bark.

Smoky's alert? Kendra quickly unzipped her coat to reach for her weapon. Her dog was sitting by a tree near the back corner of the property. The way her K9 stared at her, Kendra knew she'd alerted on a specific scent. Not an animal.

The bad guy? Someone else? A wave of apprehension washed over her as she hurried toward her K9, weapon drawn. She didn't see anyone, but that didn't mean the shooter wasn't nearby.

Just waiting to make his move.

13

After carrying his dirty dish to the kitchen, Dom headed upstairs to check out the bedrooms. If he was honest, he was procrastinating because he wasn't sure that connecting through his rerouted ISP address was the right thing to do. The fact that they kept getting found gnawed at him. As he poked his head into the rooms, he wondered about the members of his project team. Some were new to the company, which might be a good place to start.

One of the bedrooms offered a nice view of the woods and mountains rising high behind the cabin. He crossed to the window for a better look.

Watching as Kendra held her weapon up and ready as she approached Smoky who was sitting near a tree sent his pulse skyrocketing. Whirling from the window, he ran out to the balcony. "Hey, Kendra and Smoky need backup! Kendra has drawn her weapon, and they're in the backyard near the woods!"

Griff and Justin leaped up, both reaching for their respective jackets. Griff made it to the back door first, but Justin wasn't far behind. "Come, Stone," Justin called as he pulled his weapon and followed Griff outside.

Raine and Levy also ran toward the back door. Unwilling to be left out of the fray, Dom thundered down the stairs. He grabbed his coat and followed the group outside.

"Kendra!" Griff's shout echoed loudly. "Are you okay? What's going on?"

"I'm not sure." Her clear voice helped take the edge of Dom's panic. "Smoky alerted on something."

"Stay back, we'll take it from here," Justin said. Dom noticed Justin's K9, Stone, had already crossed the yard to be near Smoky. Stone sniffed the ground but didn't bark.

"Smoky is my responsibility," Kendra snapped. "I'm sticking close to my K9."

Dom quickly caught up to the rest. "What caught her attention?"

"There are footprints in the snow back here. I'm not sure who they belong to, but they're obviously recent." Kendra frowned as she turned to scan the area. "I was just about to give Smoky the search command to see if she'd continue following whatever scent she's alerted on."

"Human prints?" Raine asked. "Maybe belonging to a hunter?"

"There wouldn't be a reason for Smoky to alert on a stranger," Justin argued. "And Stone hasn't alerted. Only Smoky."

Levy looked confused. "I don't understand. What's the big deal is over a K9 alert?"

"Our dogs don't alert without a reason," Kendra explained. "Normally, we have a scent source to provide our K9s so they can find and track lost people. I didn't give Smoky a search command. She caught the scent and came running over here where there were footprints."

"She may have caught the scent of the bad guy at some point," Griff said. "I know Royal did that in the past."

"The gunman has mostly been shooting at us from his truck," Dom argued. "How could Smoky catch his scent?"

"Except for the cabin, remember?" Kendra caught his gaze. "I saw someone moving through the woods. Smoky may have picked up that person's scent."

She still held her weapon in hand, just like

everyone else. Dom hated being the only one un-armed. Kendra turned to her K9. "Are you ready, girl? Are you? Search!"

Dom wasn't sure what he expected, but he was surprised when Smoky jumped up and lowered her snout to the ground. The K9 trotted deeper into the woods, clearly following the footprints. At least to Dom, the footprints were clear, but he knew the K9 was paying more attention to a specific scent.

Kendra was hot on Smoky's heels as the dog made her way through the woods. Dom didn't hear anything beyond the wind as they followed. He re-membered how the K9 had tracked him in a similar manner, what, barely twenty-four hours ago?

It seemed like a lifetime. And he was struck by how much he would miss Kendra once this was over.

"Where is the dog taking us?" Levy asked, inter-rupting his thoughts.

"She's following the scent trail." Dom glanced at the US Marshal. "Hopefully, Smoky will lead us straight to the gunman."

"That would be nice." Levy's voice was slightly breathless, as if the guy didn't normally jog through the snow. Dom didn't either, but obviously Kendra, Justin, Raine, and Griff were all accustomed to this sort of thing.

No way did he intend to be left behind. Putting

on a burst of speed, Dom used his long legs to pass Levy and the others to catch up to Kendra.

"Are you okay?" he asked as he kept pace beside her.

She nodded, barely giving him a glance before her gaze focused on her dog. "Good girl! Search!"

From what Dom could tell, the K9 didn't need Kendra's encouragement. Smoky's high, curved tail wagged back and forth as she eagerly trotted across the snow. Then the dog abruptly slowed and turned to the right. Seeing the footprints, he scanned the horizon, wondering if the gunman was hiding someplace nearby.

Justin and Stone stayed to Kendra's left. Dom sensed that the moment Justin saw a threat, he'd leap out to confront it first to protect his sister. It was something Dom would do as well, especially if he had a weapon.

The dog disappeared from his line of sight for a long moment, then let out a sharp bark. Kendra and Justin sprinted forward, their weapons held ready. He made sure to keep up as they broke through the foliage to see what had caught Smoky's attention.

As Dom emerged, he saw Smoky sitting near what appeared to be a flattened area of snow. It took him a moment to realize they were made by a snowmobile. Everyone gathered around as Kendra bent to praise her K9. Dom noticed she didn't have her stuffed hippo; it was back at the log cabin.

"Someone was here and not that long ago." Justin's tone was grim. "I didn't hear a snowmobile, did anyone else?"

"Now that you mention it, I did hear a rumbling sound earlier." Kendra straightened. "I thought maybe it was a car on the road, but I didn't see anything."

Griff scowled. "The wind may have carried the sound away from our location."

"What makes you think these tracks are recent?" Levy asked. The marshal was bent at the torso, propping his hands on his knees. "These could have been left days ago."

"They've been made prior to the recent snowfall," Justin said. "The track marks are too clear for them to have been left prior to that."

Levy flushed, although Dom couldn't tell if he was embarrassed or just breathless. He edged closer to Justin, then nodded. "Okay, I see what you mean. These tracks would have been filled with snow if they were made yesterday."

"Exactly." Griff turned to look at Kendra. "What do you think? Should we follow these tracks to see where they go?"

"I'm not sure." Kendra grimaced and glanced at the track that disappeared in the distance. "We could, but I have the sense they're going to end at a road."

"Of course, we have to keep going," Levy argued. "We need to find this guy before he escapes again."

Justin and Griff exchanged a long look. Justin sighed. "If I were the gunman, I'd make sure the snowmobile trailer and truck were left far enough away to make it more difficult for anyone to track me on foot."

"We could call Joel, see if he wants to bring our snow machines out," Kendra suggested.

"Not sure that will help," Griff argued. "By then, this guy will for sure be long gone. If we're going, we should do that now."

"I say we keep going," Levy said. "We've come this far." For being the guy who was most out of shape compared to the others, the US Marshal was determined to push forward with the search. For once, Dom tended to agree.

"Okay, let's go." Kendra turned and broke into a jog. "Come, Smoky."

Dom quickly followed, keeping to the center of the snow machine track. The others fell into line behind him. He was impressed Justin and Griff had allowed Kendra to take the lead. He'd anticipated an argument.

Then again, this was likely a fruitless endeavor.

Everyone seemed to believe the gunman was long gone.

Except for Levy.

Nobody spoke for the next ten minutes. Kendra kept a brisk pace, with Smoky leaping through the snow beside her. Dom's energy was lagging, but he refused to slow down. If Kendra could do this, so would he.

Glancing over his shoulder, he couldn't help but notice Levy was trailing behind. Every few minutes, Raine glanced back at him. To the guy's credit, he didn't complain.

The snow machine tracks curved to the right. Another ten minutes passed before Kendra and Smoky slowed down. Dom frowned when he saw a lump of metal sitting at the side of the road.

"Kendra, wait!" He rushed forward, not wanting her anywhere near the abandoned snow machine.

"There's nobody here." The words were barely out of Kendra's mouth when Smoky reached the snowmobile, sniffed the ground around it, then let out a shrill bark.

"Was that an alert?" Justin asked, quickly joining them.

"Stay back," Griff warned. "We need to check for footprints."

Dom could see the snowmobile had been left near the edge of a rural highway. Because it had broken down? He frowned, trying to imagine the scenario.

"The footprints are crossed over, making it impossible to get a good look at them," Kendra said. "We need to see if the machine works."

Griff frowned, making a wide circle around the machine. In the time they were gathered there, looking for evidence, Levy finally caught up.

"Now what?" Levy glanced at each of them while he gasped for breath. "Why did the gunman leave it behind?"

"Let's see if it works." Before anyone could stop her, Kendra straddled the snow machine and cranked the key.

Nothing happened.

Kendra tried again. The engine still didn't turn over. She peered at the dashboard, then turned toward Justin. "It's low on fuel."

"That's odd." Justin scowled. "Anyone who rides snowmobiles on a regular basis knows enough to bring extra fuel. Especially if you're riding out in the wilderness."

"A newbie mistake?" Raine asked. "I guess it's possible."

"I don't know about that." Griff dropped to one knee to examine the ground more closely. "I almost think there are two sets of prints. Yet they're so messed up, I can't say for sure."

"You think the riders obliterated their prints on purpose?" Kendra asked.

"Has anyone . . . seen more than one . . . gunman?" Levy demanded between breaths. Dom hoped the older guy wasn't about to have the big heart attack right then and there. "Are we wrong about this? Maybe we just stumbled across a couple of people out for a joyride?"

"I have not seen two people," Kendra said firmly.

"Me either," Dom added. "Although we haven't really gotten a close look at the guy either." The only one who had was Levy himself.

"There are tire tracks on the road," Justin said, moving away from the snow machine. "But they're crisscrossed too. There isn't a clear set to verify they belong to a GMC Sierra."

Griff hurried over to see for himself. "You're right. Impossible to identify a make or model of the truck from this."

"I agree." Justin propped his hands on his hips. "They could belong to a GMC Sierra or something else."

"Maybe we should call in the crime scene techs," Levy said. "They're the experts."

"There hasn't been a crime to investigate," Raine protested. "Right now, all we have is Smoky's alert and an abandoned snow machine left behind because it ran out of fuel. We have no idea why Smoky recognized the driver's scent."

"That's true. And we can't say for sure the scent belongs to the gunman," Justin added. "For all we know, Smoky was just alerting us to the fact that someone was standing there, watching the place."

Dom frowned. He trusted Smoky's nose over just about anything or anyone. Yet he could see Raine's point. All they knew for sure was that someone had driven a truck here, dropped off a snow machine, and used it to cross the woods. That same person had then gotten off the machine and walked close enough to eyeball the cabin. Maybe the smoke wafting from the chimney had caught the snowmobiler's attention. When the snow machine failed, the driver called a friend or simply jumped into the truck to drive away.

A random innocent person or the gunman?

Either way, he wasn't convinced they should stay at the log cabin moving forward. And from the dark expression on Justin's face, Kendra's brother shared his concern.

"Come, Smoky." Kendra called her K9 from the snow machine. She felt bad she didn't have the stuffed hippo, but in truth, she wasn't sure she should reward Smoky for a job well done. At least, not when she had no idea who Smoky had alerted on.

"I don't believe in coincidences," Justin muttered as Kendra turned to head back toward the cabin.

Kendra sighed. "I don't either, but tell me this, why would the gunman go to all this trouble to find us just to jump into his truck and drive away?"

"I don't know." Justin scowled.

"If you ask me, this entire situation doesn't make any sense." Dom came up on her other side. She had to admit, he'd done an admirable job of keeping up. "I don't like it."

"That makes three of us," Griff said.

"Four," Raine added. She glanced over her shoulder to where Levy was trudging along several paces behind them. "May as well make it five. I know Levy doesn't like any of this either."

Kendra glanced at her K9. As if reading her mind, Justin nodded, and said, "Always trust your dog."

"I do trust her," Kendra said. "I'm just not sure what she's trying to tell me."

"That's our fault, not hers." Justin's expression softened. "We'll figure it out."

"I hope so." Kendra sighed, praying that knowledge wouldn't come too late. "She's never done this before."

"That's what Joel said back when Royal did the same thing." Justin shrugged. "Our K9s are well trained and eager to please."

Her brother wasn't telling her anything she didn't already know.

Griff lengthened his stride to join them, peering down at his phone. "I was able to get the VIN number off the snowmobile," he announced. "We'll run this through the database, see who the machine belongs to."

"You did?" Dom looked surprised. "I didn't know they had VIN numbers."

"They do, same as four-wheelers and other motorized vehicles." Griff shrugged. "Let's hope this one wasn't stolen. Although that may explain why there wasn't much gas in the tank."

"How did the guy steal a snowmobile and get it all the way out here?" Dom asked.

"Could have managed to get it into the bed of the Sierra," Justin said.

"He'd need a ramp," Kendra said. "Unless the two of them picked it up."

"Not easy, but not impossible." Griff shrugged. "It's just a theory. We'll know more when we get back to the log cabin."

Kendra tried to imagine the gunman finding a snowmobile to steal, getting it into the truck, and dropping it off. "I think the machine was on a trailer."

They all fell silent as they retraced their steps. When the snowmobile tracks gave way to the footprints, Kendra knew they were finally getting close.

"Why does it seem to take longer to get back?" Dom asked.

"Adrenaline spurred us on. Now we have nothing but sheer will to push forward." She managed a grim smile. "At least, that's how it works for SAR missions."

"Makes sense." He glanced at her. "I trust you and your dog, Kendra. I believe she alerted on the footprints and the snow machine for a reason."

"Thanks." She was touched by his comment considering Dom hadn't been around the Sullivan K9s until recently.

"How much farther?" Levy's voice was weak. Turning around, Kendra could see the older man was struggling to get through the deep snow. Having snowshoes would help, but she doubted Levy knew how to use them.

After consulting her GPS, she said, "One more mile."

Levy groaned.

Another fifteen minutes later, Kendra slowed her pace. They'd reached the trees where Smoky had first alerted. The back of the cabin was in view, and she frowned at the light shining from the kitchen window.

"What's wrong?" Dom asked, sensing her concern.

"I don't remember using any of the lights." She turned to eye Justin and Griff who were close behind her. "Did either of you leave a light on?"

"No." Instantly, Griff had his weapon in hand. "Someone may have gone inside while we were out here."

"Stay back," Justin added. "Griff and I will clear the house."

Kendra tried not to sigh. The guys were always acting as if she hadn't a clue how to use a gun. Sure, Griff was a fed, but Justin wasn't.

"I'm with you," Griff said.

"What are we, chopped liver?" Raine demanded. "We're all armed and know how to protect ourselves."

"Dom's not armed, although he is a good shot," Kendra said. "No reason we all need to stay behind."

"Just let us take the lead," Griff insisted. "We may need you to head out to get backup."

"Backup?" Levy finally caught up to them. "I doubt the gunman is inside. He wouldn't be foolish enough to turn on a light."

Kendra grabbed Dom's arm, holding him back so the others could approach the cabin first. Dom's frustrated expression spoke volumes. Although she was relieved he didn't shake off her grip.

"Someone must have a spare weapon I can use," he said in a low tone. "I hate feeling useless."

"Not that I'm aware of." She watched as Justin and Griff split up, one heading around to the front, the other lingering in the back. Raine, for all her tough talk, stayed back as if to guard her and Dom. Justin's K9, Stone, stayed at Raine's side, although it seemed as if the dog wanted to follow Justin. Even Levy hung back, as if sensing the younger men were better suited to take on a threat.

A few tense minutes later, Justin went into the house through the back door. Raine took one step, as if she wanted to follow, but then stopped.

For a long moment nobody moved. Kendra imagined the two men clearing the cabin. Was she wrong about the light? Maybe they had left it on.

But she didn't think so.

Another long minute later, Justin stepped back outside. He didn't look happy but gestured for them to head over.

Raine and Stone led the way. Kendra, Dom, and Smoky were right behind her. Levy once again was the last one to arrive. A wave of warm air greeted Kendra as stepped across the threshold.

Smoky snaked around her, going farther inside. Then her K9 let out a sharp bark.

Kendra's muscles went tense.

"Hey, Smoky, do you remember me?" The female voice was not what Kendra had anticipated. She hurried forward, her jaw dropping in shock when she saw Jennifer Hutchins standing in the kitchen. Her last SAR mission involved finding a lost woman not far from the Redwood Motel in Greybull.

And now Jennifer was standing in their log cabin.

"Hi, Kendra." Jennifer looked relieved to see her as she tucked a strand of her long dark hair behind her ear. "I'm so glad to see you. I tried to tell these guys you'd remember me, but they didn't believe me. At least Smoky remembered me, didn't you, girl? Huh?" Jennifer bent to stroke the dog's fur.

"What are you doing here, Jennifer?" Kendra couldn't tear her gaze from the tall dark-haired woman. "How did you know I was here?"

"I didn't know you were here, but I need gas for my snow machine." Jennifer cocked her head to the side. "Did you find it?"

"We did," Griff answered. He took a step closer to Jennifer. In sync with Griff, Justin did the same from the other side. "But you need to answer Kendra's question. How did you know she was here?"

"I didn't!" Jennifer's tone turned indignant. She

looked from Griff to Justin, then back to Kendra. "Why is everyone acting as if I've done something terrible? I drove past the cabin, saw the cars, and came in to ask for help. That's all."

No way. Kendra couldn't quite explain why the woman's words didn't ring true. Finding Jennifer inside the safe house explained Smoky's alert. Her dog would have recognized Jennifer's scent from their previous search, especially since that was only a few days ago. Even if Kendra hadn't given her K9 the search command.

Yet having Jennifer Hutchins show up here at a federal safe house did not make sense. She glanced at Justin who seemed to understand her concern.

"Look, if you don't want to give me some gas to fill up the snow machine, that's fine." Jennifer tossed her hair, as if annoyed. "I figured since you helped find me when I was lost a few days ago, you'd help again. But I guess I was wrong."

Jennifer's comment only deepened her mistrust. She'd just said she didn't know Kendra would be there. Now she was using their relationship as a reason she'd help? No way. "Griff and Justin? Grab her."

Without hesitation, both men leaped forward to snag Jennifer's arms. The woman's eyes widened in alarm. "Get your hands off me! What are you doing? I came for help, nothing more."

"She's part of this." Kendra gave Smoky the hand signal to come. Her dog wheeled away from Jennifer, coming to sit at the heel position. "I'm not sure how or why, but she's involved."

"Involved in what? What are you talking about?" Jennifer tried to sound confused, but her narrowed eyes reflected the truth.

Jennifer Hutchins was involved in the attacks against her and Dominic. But Kendra didn't think she was the gunman. There had been two sets of prints on the ground outside, and that made her think Jennifer wasn't working alone. "Where is he?"

"I don't know what you're talking about!" Jennifer's shrill voice held a note of panic. "Let me go!"

"Where is he?" Kendra took a step closer. "You're not smart enough to have done this on your own. Where is he?"

Jennifer stopped struggling, looked away, and clamped her lips together tightly. Clearly, she was done talking.

Kendra turned toward Dom. "We need to get out of here."

Despite his dazed expression, he nodded. As he reached for the laptop computer, a loud explosion just outside the log cabin rocked the earth, sending them all tumbling to the floor.

14

"Let's go. We need to get out of here!" Dom blinked, staring up at Levy's grim expression hovering over him. One minute he was standing and talking to Kendra, the next he was on the floor. The older man yanked on his arm, trying to get Dom up on his feet. Ears ringing from the blast, he managed to stand. "Hurry," Levy urged.

Somehow, Dom still held the laptop. How he hadn't dropped it was a mystery, but he tucked it under his arm and took a few stumbling steps toward the back door as Levy pulled him forward. He wasn't sure what had happened, but he knew it was bad. It was important to get away from the safe house. As that thought formed, he abruptly stopped, resisting Levy. "Wait. Where's Kendra?"

"Her brother has her. Hurry!" Levy yanked hard on his arm. "There's no time to waste."

Doing his best to gather his scattered thoughts, Dom followed Levy through the house. The US Marshal already had the back door open and was practically shoving him through it. The blast of cold air helped clear his mind.

Why did Jennifer look so familiar? Obviously, Kendra assumed the woman was involved in this mess somehow, but he wasn't sure how or why. He didn't recognize her first name, had Kendra mentioned her last name? He didn't think so. Yet there was something about Jennifer that tugged at his memory. An elusive thought that hung suspended in the back of his mind, just out of reach.

Levy continued pulling him away from the house. Dom abruptly stopped when he noticed nobody else had come with them. He planted his feet in the snow, refusing to budge. "Wait. I need to find Kendra!"

"She's not my responsibility. You are." Levy's voice was hard. "It's my job to keep you safe."

"I'm not leaving without her." Dom pulled free of Levy's grip. As much as he appreciated the guy's determination to get him out of harm's way, he wasn't about to leave Kendra behind.

Not now, not ever.

His grim resolve had him turning back toward the house. Why hadn't Kendra and the others followed them outside? What was the cause of the explosion anyway?

"Stop!" Levy's sharp command had him turning toward the US Marshal. His jaw dropped in shock when his gaze landed on the gun in his hand. The gun pointed directly at his chest. "You're coming with me."

For a moment, Dom didn't understand. Was Levy's job so important he'd force Dom to go with him at gunpoint?

No, that wasn't it. A grim realization washed over him. Levy was a part of this after all.

"Move." The gun in Levy's hand didn't waver. "I'll shoot you here and now if necessary. I'll tell the others you went crazy, lashing out at me, forcing me to defend myself."

Dom swallowed hard. "Kendra will never believe that."

Levy shrugged. "Doesn't matter as long as Griff and Raine buy my story."

Was he right? Dom didn't know Kendra's family very well, other than they were super protective of her. Would they believe her over a US Marshal? Maybe not.

Casting one last glance over his shoulder, Dom

reluctantly moved forward. Now that he knew Levy was involved, going along with him might keep Kendra safe. Unless, of course, Levy intended to return to the Sullivan ranch later to finish the job.

He'd need to find a way to escape. How, he wasn't sure. If only he'd insisted on having a weapon!

"Faster," Levy ordered. "We need to distance ourselves from the rest."

"Why are you doing this?" Dom strove to remain calm. Getting away from the log cabin was fine with him. The farther he could get Levy away from Kendra and the others, the better. But he wasn't going to give up without a fight. No matter what. "Is this about money? Or something else?"

"Shut up and keep walking." Levy kept his distance, the nose of the gun still trained on his chest. "Hurry. Our ride will be waiting for us."

"What ride?" He strove to keep Levy talking. "Who's waiting for us? Bartoli? Is he the man who hired you?"

"I thought you and the Sullivans knew more than you did," Levy admitted. "I guess that idiot didn't pass along as much information as we feared."

"So why not let us go?" Even as Dom asked the question, he knew it was too late for that. Too many

people had already died over this—whatever
this was.

"Hurry." Levy's expression was stern. "We
should reach the road soon. It curves around,
making it easier to hide our backup plan." The US
Marshal smirked. "You never suspected me after I
played my role perfectly, did you?"

"No, I didn't." Dom wanted to kick himself for
letting his guard down. Yet the gunfire that erupted
outside their previous rental property had convinced him the guy was in the clear. Now he knew
that was nothing more than a setup. A way to convince them all that Levy was one of the good guys.

He wasn't. But that was his problem now. Dom
pushed forward, hoping and praying Kendra would
be safe with him and Levy out of the picture.

At least for now.

As they continued walking, Dom realized Levy
was right about the road. Through a pair of towering trees, he saw a large dark truck sitting off on
the side of the snowy highway. He was too far away
to say for sure, but he figured it was the GMC Sierra
with the snow-covered license plate.

Driven, no doubt, by the relentless gunman
who'd been tracking him since he arrived at the
Redwood Motel. It seemed like eons ago that he'd
been targeted near his vehicle. Was his truck still at
the motel? Probably.

Kendra had mentioned doing a search and rescue mission near the Redwood, finding the lost woman who turned out to be Jennifer. What was her last name? Why couldn't he figure out where he'd seen her before?

"Move it!" Levy's sharp tone made Dom realize his steps had slowed to a stop. Now that they'd gotten this close to their destination, he was loath to get inside the truck. He preferred being outside than crammed inside the vehicle. Besides, getting in with two armed men did not seem like a smart move. "I prefer to keep you alive but will shoot if you keep stalling."

"I, uh"—Dom turned toward Levy—"can we talk about this? I swear I'm not a threat to you or to Bartoli."

"How's this for talking? Get in the truck!" Levy lifted the gun, holding it with two hands so that the muzzle was pointed at his face. Normally, staring at a loaded weapon this close would have frozen Dom with fear. He'd never been shot and wasn't eager to try the experience now. Yet oddly, a sense of calm washed over him. Maybe Kendra's faith in God had rubbed off on him, because he wasn't afraid of this man at all.

If he died today, he hoped and prayed he could take Levy down with him.

"Dominic!" The faint sound of Kendra calling

his name offered the distraction he needed. When Levy glanced around to find the source of the shout, Dom lunged forward, swinging the computer down with both hands, striking Levy's wrists with a loud crack. He was taller than the marshal, and having longer limbs worked to his advantage.

Screaming in pain and fury, Levy dropped the gun. Without hesitation, Dom shoved Levy, sending him tumbling backward, before turning and sprinting toward the woods. There wasn't a second to waste. Hunching his shoulders, Dom silently prayed as he ran, his long stride taking him quickly toward safety, even as he fully anticipated a bullet from the gunman inside the truck would strike the center of his back at any moment.

Killing him.

The crack of gunfire was loud enough to make him stumble. The gunman must have gotten out of the truck or maybe Levy had pulled himself together long enough to find the dropped weapon. Either way, it took Dom a moment to realize he hadn't been hit. Putting on a burst of speed, he disappeared behind the trees.

Yet even then, he didn't stop. Feet slipping in the snow, he continued moving deeper into the woods, angling away from the log cabin. Primarily, his goal was to use the thick woods for cover, to make it difficult for the gunman to hit him. But more importantly, he needed to draw the killer away from Kendra and her family.

Levy wanted him. Alive or dead. Either for revenge or money, or both. The longer he could keep Kendra and her siblings out of this mess, the better.

Yet he also knew that much like that first night, he was leaving tracks in the snow. It wouldn't take that long for Levy and the gunman to find him.

Still, he pushed forward. Maybe he'd buy Kendra and the others a little time to figure out what was going on, before he was silenced for good.

Dear Lord Jesus, keep Kendra and the others safe in Your care!

"Dominic!" Kendra shouted Dom's name as loud as she could.

"Easy, we'll find him," Justin said in a low voice.

Would they? She shook her head, fighting a wave of helplessness. "Levy's a part of this." Kendra scowled at her brother. Griff and Raine had Jennifer's wrists bound behind her back and tied to a chair, but there was no sign of Levy and Dom. The explosion had sent them all tumbling to the floor, but thankfully, Griff had held on to Jennifer. They had one perp in custody, but there were others. Including Levy. Once Justin had glanced outside to see there was nobody around, they'd gone out the back. It was the only way Levy could have gotten Dom out of there.

"The gunman targeted him too," Justin protested. "Maybe he just wanted to get Dom to safety?"

"No way. He's involved. I think the shooting at the previous house was a cover-up. Levy suspected we were onto him, so he changed tactics. And we bought his *I'm innocent* act, didn't we?" She raked her gaze over the area. "The only way Jennifer could have found us here at the FBI safe house was if Levy told her where we were. Abandoning the snow machine was a setup as well. Maybe because she heard Smoky's bark and knew the gig was up. Her mistake was thinking we'd fall for her innocent act the way we did with Levy."

Justin grimaced and nodded. "Okay, I admit, it's strange we were found here. I'm on board with treating Levy as a hostile enemy."

"Don't forget, the gunman is still at large too." Kendra's pulse raced as she tried to remain calm. She wondered why Jennifer had gotten herself lost a few days ago, requiring Kendra to find her. Was that to make sure Smoky didn't see her as a threat? Maybe. But that had ended up working against her. Not something to think about now, though. They needed to find Dom. She looked at Smoky, doing her best to inject enthusiasm into her tone. "Are you ready? Search! Search Dominic!"

Smoky wheeled around and led the way, crossing the backyard where multiple sets of footprints marred the snow. Kendra ignored the footprints. They'd all walked around in the back, so following a specific set of prints now to find Dom and Levy would be impossible.

Smoky's keen nose was their only hope of finding Dom. How far could Levy have taken him anyway?

She was afraid they may already be too late. Once Levy had Dominic in a moving vehicle, their chances of finding him dropped dramatically.

When gunfire rang out, Kendra's heart lodged in her chest. Was he hit? Or worse, dead? "Dom! Where are you?"

There was nothing but silence.

"Maybe we should spread out," Justin suggested.

"Do what you think is best." She'd used Smoky to find Dominic before, and her K9 would follow the scent now. "Smoky will find him."

Justin frowned but didn't argue. Rather than leaving her, he stayed close to her side as she hurried behind her K9. Smoky was clearly on Dominic's scent, alternating between sniffing along the snow and up in the air. When Smoky picked up her pace, her tail wagging back and forth, Kendra's heart filled with hope.

Was Dominic on foot? If so, she knew Smoky would find him. If not . . .

No, she wasn't going there. She broke into a run, keeping pace with her dog as she silently prayed. *Please, Lord Jesus, help us find Dominic in time!*

Smoky abruptly veered off, heading deeper into the woods. Kendra's steps floundered, doubt seeping in. Was Smoky on the right path? Or had she somehow gotten sidetracked?

"Keep going." Justin's encouragement was just what she needed. "Smoky is on his scent."

Desperate to believe that, she pushed forward, ignoring her exhaustion. Her fluffy dog zigzagged through the trees with seemingly boundless energy. Kendra noticed there was only a single set of footprints in the snow now. They were also spread far apart, more so than what she could manage. They had to belong to Dominic. She could easily imagine him running full out.

Somehow, he'd gotten away from Levy!

Kendra wanted to call out to him but held her tongue. Dom may have escaped, but someone had fired at him.

Levy? The gunman? Both?

She glanced back at Justin. "You should go back to Griff and Raine. They may be in danger."

"Not happening." Her brother scowled. "They're cops. They'll handle it."

Arguing would be useless. The only person more stubborn than a Sullivan was another Sullivan.

Smoky disappeared behind a large evergreen tree. Then she heard the sharp bark as Smoky alerted.

A fresh surge of adrenaline pushed Kendra forward. She ran around the tree, stopping abruptly when she saw Dominic kneeling beside Smoky.

"Good girl," she managed as she closed the distance between them.

Dominic straightened and came to meet her, sweeping her into a big hug. He held her close for long seconds until Justin and Stone appeared.

She wanted to protest when Dom let her go. But then he got straight to the point. "I'm glad you're here, but there's no time to waste. Levy is involved. He had the gunman waiting in the black GMC Sierra down the road."

"Did he give you any hint as to why? What's his relationship to Bartoli? Or does he have another motive?" Justin asked.

Dom shook his head. "No, but I assume it's money. Where are Griff and Raine?"

"They're guarding Jennifer." Kendra bent to praise her K9, wishing she had grabbed the stuffed hippo. She'd have to do more training with Smoky now that these two recent searches hadn't been properly rewarded. Although based on Smoky's leaping around in joy, her K9 didn't seem to mind not getting her toy.

Smoky ran off, leaping and playing with Stone. Kendra figured that would have to be enough of a reward for now.

"That Jennifer looks familiar, but I can't place her." Dom's brow furrowed as he struggled to remember. "I wish I could say when I met her. Not that it matters anymore. The most important thing is to make sure Griff and Raine know Levy's dirty."

"Texting Griff now," Justin said, his thumbs flying across his phone screen. "Although I think they've already figured that out for themselves."

Kendra arched a brow. "Really? Then why did I have to convince you about Levy's involvement in this?"

Justin shrugged. "I was leaning that way but thought it was strange that he'd risk being shot by the gunman just to insert himself into the group."

"Yeah, we'll it's clear he wants to kill me," Dom said bluntly. "For whatever reason, he wanted to get me out of there. Forced me to leave at gunpoint."

"I'm surprised he didn't just shoot you and be done with it." Justin frowned. "Easier that way."

Kendra shot an infuriating look at her brother,

although what he said was true. A shiver that had nothing to do with the freezing temps danced down her spine. It was scary how Levy had almost succeeded in eliminating Dominic. And the danger wasn't over yet.

"Well, he said he'd prefer to take me alive but would settle for dead," Dom admitted,

She managed a reassuring smile. "Thankfully, you were smart enough to get away. You're safe now. But we need to go back to the log cabin."

"What if Levy and the gunman are still out there?" Dom didn't move an inch, but his gaze continuously tracked back and forth as if expecting the men to show up at any moment. "I don't want you anywhere near him, Kendra. He won't hesitate to shoot you to get to me."

"I know, but we outnumber him," she pointed out. "That's probably why he tried to get you into the truck alone. Separating you from us was his best chance of trying to come up with an alternate plan."

"I guess," Dom said with a frown.

She reached out to touch his arm. "It's not like we have another option but to go back." She tipped her head toward the landscape beyond. There was nothing but woods and snow for as far as they could see. "The dogs are having a blast out here, but we can't hang out here in the cold forever."

Still, Dom didn't move. "What about texting Griff and Raine? I'm worried we'll walk into a trap."

She shrugged and glanced at her brother. "You told them about Levy, right? Did either of them respond?"

"Not yet." Justin's scowl deepened. "I hope they're not in trouble. I agree, it's time for us to get out of here."

"Sounds good." She turned toward the dogs. "Smoky, come." Her K9 turned and bounded to her side. Stone ran toward Justin, as if anticipating he was next.

"I'll take the lead." Justin unzipped his coat and pulled his weapon. Kendra mirrored his action, although her gun was heavy in her hand. Chase would be disappointed in how often she forgot to reach for her gun.

"Look out!" The shout was punctuated by the sharp crack of gunfire. Something struck her hard in the back, sending her face-first into the snow. Kendra's breath whooshed from her chest as her heart thundered in her ears.

What was going on?

More gunfire rang out. Kendra struggled to free herself of the heavy weight on top of her. She needed to find Smoky! What if her K9 was hit?

"Stay down." Dom's voice was near her ear. Realizing he was the one who'd jumped on top of her helped a little, but she was still desperate to save her dog.

"Smoky!" Her hoarse cry was muffled by snow. She lifted her head, trying to breathe as she searched for her K9. Her dog was half covered in snow, making her blend into their surroundings. The K9 was growling low in her throat, staring at something in the distance. Levy? Or the gunman? For all she knew, both men may have joined the fray.

Where was her gun? Kendra almost sobbed when she realized she'd dropped it when Dom barreled into her. She was failing miserably at this and hated to admit Chase had been right to be upset with her for embarking on this plan of protecting Dominic on her own.

That thought made her wonder about Justin. She twisted her head to see better. Her brother was sprawled on his stomach just a few feet away. She watched him for a long second, panicking when she realized he wasn't moving. Stone was stretched out beside him in the snow, his nose inches from Justin's face. Her heart squeezed painfully as she feared the worst.

Had Justin been killed?

They needed to do something! Frantic now, Kendra bucked against Dom's body lying on top of her. "Get off, get off!" She searched the snow for her weapon. "We need to save him!"

"Raine is here," Dom said, his voice irrationally calm. "Stay down."

She didn't want to stay down! Knowing Raine had arrived brought some measure of relief, but that wasn't good enough if her brother was bleeding to death. Changing tactics, she abruptly wiggled backward. Her movement took Dom by surprise, and Kendra was able to get out from beneath him. Finally free, she pushed herself to her hands and knees, crawling through the snow toward her brother. She reached for his foot, grabbing his ankle and shaking it hard. "Justin! Talk to me! Are you hurt?"

To her surprise, he lifted his head and turned to look at her. Now that she was close, she could see he had one arm wrapped around his K9. "It's a flesh wound. Get down!"

A flesh wound! She belatedly noticed a sprinkling of red droplets of blood across the snow near his right arm. Maybe it wasn't serious, but Justin was right-handed. And that meant he couldn't return fire.

She needed her weapon, and fast! The report of gunfire had stopped, but she was afraid it would start again any second. Especially if Raine was facing off against two men.

Keeping her head down, she turned to crawl back toward Dominic. "We need to find my gun," she whispered.

Dom pushed up to his knees and dragged his hands through the snow. His arms moved like a giant windmill, and if she wasn't scared to death, she might have laughed. A moment later, he triumphantly held up her gun. It was wet and covered with snow, but that didn't matter. She knew it would still fire if she could manage to hit what she was aiming at.

A big if, under the circumstances.

"Thanks." She held out her hand, but he shook his head.

"I've got it." Dom's expression was grim. "You need to stay behind me."

Frustrated, she almost snapped. Then she realized Smoky was standing with her nose to the air, sniffing intently. She crawled behind Dom, then called to her K9. "Smoky, come."

Thankfully, her dog obeyed her command. Dom was still on his knees, but he was so tall that he may as well have been standing upright. She wrapped one arm around Smoky, pulling the dog close, then grabbed the back of his jacket with the other, needing the physical connection to face whatever threat lurked in the distance.

"Kendra? Justin? Are you okay?" Raine called.

"I'm fine." Kendra relaxed her grip on Dom's coat.

"I'm okay too," Justin said. Looking around Dom's back, she realized Justin had pushed himself up to his feet. The way he cradled his right arm across his chest indicated he was hurt more than he let on.

"Good. I have the gunman in custody." Raine's voice rang with satisfaction. "But there's no sign of Levy."

Kendra grimaced, knowing Levy must have taken the opportunity to escape. The coward.

"Who is the shooter?" Dom asked. "Do you recognize him?"

"Never seen him before in my life." Raine stepped out from behind the trees, pushing a man dressed in black. Kendra didn't recognize him either, but one thing was clear. He wasn't a younger white guy, the way Levy had claimed. The US Marshal had lied about that. The man Raine had in custody had darker skin and black hair, almost as if he were from Romania. Or maybe some other Eastern European country.

Was he involved in the South African cartel?

"I recognize him," Dominic said, breaking the silence. "His name is Jake Hutchins. He's my second-in-command at Data Intelligence Services."

Hutchins? The last name clicked in her mind.

This guy was married or related to Jennifer Hutchins. Likely married, as Jennifer had fair skin.

Stunned, she realized the cartel had infiltrated Dominic's company. No wonder every time he'd used the computer they were found. This guy had likely learned the technique from Dom himself.

The immediate threat was over, but Kendra knew they still needed to find Levy before he struck again.

15

———

Dom stared at Jake Hutchins feeling sick. The guy had worked for him for a full year, and Dom had taught him everything he knew. To his detriment. Obviously, Jake had been the one to keep finding him, despite his attempt to cover his electronic trail. Dom knew he should have suspected someone close to him was involved.

Worse, he now remembered where he'd seen Jennifer. He kicked himself for not realizing who she was. Jennifer worked in the Data Intelligence Services human resources department. In fact, Jennifer had encouraged him to hire Jake.

The fact that they'd worked together to try to kill him and Kendra was a bitter pill to swallow. He'd trusted Jake. Had left him in charge while he was going on vacation. And Jake had taken full advantage of the situation. In fact, he'd told Jake he was heading to the Redwood Motel in Greybull.

"Why?" Dom stared his team leader, who was standing beside Raine with his wrists cuffed behind his back. "Why did you try to kill us?"

Jake avoided his gaze and didn't answer.

"He has the right to remain silent," Raine drawled. "But I am hoping that we can convince him to cooperate by giving us information on Levy and Bartoli in exchange for a lighter sentence."

If that was something Jake was considering, he didn't let on. The way he stared off in the distance, Dom wasn't sure what was going through his mind. The only good thing was that Jake wasn't getting his big payday as he'd planned.

The jerk.

Kendra wrapped her arm around Dom's waist. Her support was sweet, but he knew that he'd been played for a fool, by both Jake and Jennifer. It made him feel bad because his blind spot had almost cost Kendra her life. "I take it the Hutchins's are related?"

"Husband and wife." Dom forced the comment through clenched teeth. "At least, that's what they claimed. I'm not even sure those are their real names."

"Jake Hutchins is his name, according to his ID," Raine said. "I have a feeling they're in this for the money."

"Maybe he'll talk to save his wife?" Kendra suggested.

"I wouldn't give him that much credit." Dom scowled and stepped away from her. Now that the immediate threat was over, he passed her weapon back. She took it with a nod of thanks. "We need to find Levy. He's likely in the black Sierra GMC truck."

"I've alerted Griff about that. I'm sure he's called that in by now." Raine gave Jake a small push. "Let's get back to the log cabin. Justin, I need to check your injury."

"I'm fine." Justin waved off his wife's concern, but by the way he cradled his arm against his chest, Dom suspected the wound hurt worse than he was letting on. His K9, Stone, stayed close to his side, as if the dog understood he was hurt too.

"Where's Trevor when we need him?" Kendra muttered as she slid her gun into her belt holster. "He's the EMT."

Dom tried to take heart in knowing that Justin wasn't hurt that badly. He glanced at Jake, wondering if his IT specialist felt even an ounce of remorse.

Nah, he wasn't buying it. Jake's stoic expression indicated he wasn't ready to cooperate.

At least, not yet. Maybe after spending a few weeks behind bars, he'd sing a different tune.

"You can stay silent, as is your right," Raine said as they walked through the snow back toward the log cabin. "But I have you on attempted murder, as I witnessed you shooting Justin. Once I process your weapon and match the shell casings with those we've recovered at other crime scenes, you'll be looking at several attempted murder charges. Including the attempted murder of a federal agent."

"Griff will press charges," Kendra said. "The same way Dom and I will."

"We'll get your wife on accessory to attempted murder," Raine went on. "Maybe she'll cooperate for a shorter sentence."

"She's just as guilty," Dom said harshly. "No way did Jake do this alone. He might be the tech expert and the main shooter, but she helped him every step of the way. And let's not forget someone caused Helen Gingrass's accident. Probably Jennifer."

Jake turned to glare at him as if he'd guessed right. Dom held his gaze, hoping he'd crack, but after a long second, Jake looked away.

They made the rest of the trip back to the log cabin in silence. Dom glanced back over his shoulder frequently, expecting Levy to jump out to shoot them at any second. The guy may have taken off to save himself, but that didn't mean he wouldn't come after Dom or Kendra again.

That thought made him frown. Why would he?

Levy had to know the Sullivans suspected him by now. And why hadn't the US Marshal killed him when he had a chance? Why try to get him into the truck? Why had he attempted to take him alive? Once Levy had separated him away from Kendra and the others, he should have put a bullet in Dom's brain. After all, that's what he'd threatened to do every step of the way.

The Krugerrand.

Dom abruptly stopped, causing Kendra to bump into him from behind. She stepped to his side, looking up at him. "Are you okay? Is something wrong?"

"I'm fine." He gave himself a mental shake forced himself to keep walking. Yeah, the more he thought about Levy hauling him toward the truck, the more convinced he was that there was more to this than Stuart Ramsey's confession.

This nightmare wasn't just about a simple confession. Levy had thought Ramsey told them more than he had, but it wasn't just that information that started this. It was about the Krugerrand. Coins that Bartoli might not have realized were in his father's possession until Stuart had given his to his hospice nurse. That was enough to raise concerns about where Stuart had gotten it. They must have assumed Stuart had taken the coin from his father, and they must have thought there were more.

A lot more.

Had his father taken the Krugerrand on the plane? In theory, it made sense that his father would keep the coins close. Yet if that was the case, the coins were likely scattered across the Bighorn Mountains like the rest of the plane debris.

Yet somehow, Dom didn't think so. He had to consider the fact that his father could have hidden the Krugerrand somewhere within the house, the hangar, or buried on the property. He'd gone through his dad's things after his death, but that had been more of a clearing-out process. Getting rid of his father's clothing and other personal belongings. He'd gone through all the boxes and closets, but he hadn't searched for hidden coins.

There was only one way to find out if there were more Krugerrand. He needed to get back to Montana.

Dazed, he followed the others into the house. It looked the same as before, minus a few pictures that had fallen off the wall after the explosion.

"Sit down, Justin. I'll look at your wound." Raine pushed Jake Hutchins toward Griff. "Keep this guy away from his wife, Jennifer. We can't allow them to communicate in any way."

Griff arched a brow and nodded. "No problem. But what happened to Justin?"

"I'm fine." Justin dropped into a chair, still

cradling his arm across his chest. "It's a flesh wound."

"We won't know that it's only a flesh wound until we examine it," Raine argued. "You can drop the tough guy act."

Griff escorted Jennifer into one of the bedrooms, then came back for Jake, taking him to a different room. Dom wished he could badger the couple with questions, but he understood the need to follow procedure. He wasn't a cop, but if he interfered with Griff and Raine, he could ruin everything.

Instead, he turned toward Justin. "Do we know what exploded outside?"

"A pipe bomb." Justin grimaced as Raine pulled his coat off to see his arm. "My take is that it was used as a diversion."

"A diversion that worked." Dom grimly remembered how Levy had used the explosion to get him out of the cabin. "Are the vehicles damaged?"

"Only one, Levy's. The other two seem okay." Justin reached down with his uninjured arm to stroke Stone, before shrugging out of his shirt. "Why?"

"I need to go." The words came from Dom's mouth before he realized what he was about to say.

"What? You can't leave." Kendra frowned. Her K9 sat at her side, clearly waiting for another opportunity to play the search game. "Levy is still out there."

"I know." Levy didn't matter as much as his need to get back to his place. If he found more Krugerrand, he'd know the coins were the reason he'd been ruthlessly tracked and nearly killed.

Along with Kendra and her family. Innocent people who'd only tried to help him.

"The Cody police are on the way," Griff said. "They'll want your statement, Dom, before you go."

He nodded, but sticking around wasn't high on his list of things to do. Kendra had her key fob, but Justin had just removed his coat. Dom took the jacket and surreptitiously slipped his hand into the pocket for the key fob as he moved it to the other chair.

"See?" Justin peered at the bleeding gash on his arm. "I told you it was just a flesh wound."

"I'm glad." Raine kissed him, then went to work cleaning the wound.

Dom swallowed hard and turned away. "I'm heading out to see if the police are here yet." Without waiting for anyone to respond, he walked outside. The previously untouched and glistening snow in the front yard was now littered with branches, twigs, and pine needle debris from the trees around them. The pipe bomb had left its mark.

The sirens were loud enough to indicate the police were on the way. Dom clicked the fob, found Justin's SUV, and slid in behind the wheel. He levered the seat back as far as possible to make room for his long legs. As he started the engine, the passenger door opened. Smoky jumped in first, followed by Kendra.

He glared at her. "You can't come with me."

"This is a Sullivan SUV, so yeah, I can." She urged Smoky into the back seat. "Don't bother arguing, that's a waste of time. If you're going, so am I."

Dom didn't like it. But she was right. They were wasting time. He hit the gas and headed out to the highway, silently praying Justin, Raine, and Griff would forgive him.

⁓

"WHAT'S GOING ON, DOMINIC?" Kendra broke the long silence as Dom navigated the highway. She would have rather had Smoky in the back crate area, but he had chosen to jump into Justin's car rather than drive her own. "Why are you heading back to Billings?"

He didn't answer for a long moment. "I almost got you and your brother killed." He shot her a quick glance, his expression grim. "And for what? A handful of gold coins?"

She frowned, then understood. "You think this is about the Krugerrand."

"Yeah." He sighed. "Don't you see? Stuart Ramsey's confession started this, but it was the Krugerrand he'd given to Helen that ramped up the danger. Bartoli must have figured out that my father had Krugerrand. For all we know, my dad stole it."

"I'm sure he didn't steal it." Even as she said the words, though, she realized it was possible. Why else would Gary Lakeland have kept the Krugerrand for so many years? Or had he used some along the way? Maybe he'd use some of the gold to support his charter business.

"I didn't know my father at all." Dom's expression was harsh. "I have no idea what he was capable of."

"If your father did take some Krugerrand, it was only to help secure a future for you." Kendra strove to sound positive. "Don't judge him for wanting to keep you safe."

Dom shook his head. "I don't know what to think. Other than I almost got you killed."

"I'm fine and so is Justin." She reached out to touch his arm. He glanced at her hand, then shook her off. She tried to hide the flash of hurt. "This isn't your fault."

He shrugged without saying anything. Kendra stared blindly out the passenger-side window. She didn't appreciate Dom keeping an emotional distance from her. As if they hadn't worked together to survive over the past twenty-four hours.

As if she hadn't fallen in love with him.

Talk about a stupid move on her part. She knew better than to open herself up to heartache. It wasn't as if Dominic would pick up his life and move to the Sullivan ranch.

Maybe she could offer to move to Billings?

The idea filled her with sadness. She'd miss her family.

The almost two-hour drive back to Billings, Montana, passed with excruciating slowness. Every time she tried to talk, Dom responded with one-word answers. By the time Dominic drove into the driveway of what she assumed was his father's home, she'd wished she'd stayed back at the log cabin.

Dom barely looked at her as he slid out of the car. Feeling like a barnacle he longed to scrape off, she called Smoky from the car and followed him inside.

"Nice place." She wasn't surprised he kept the place neat and tidy. Smoky sniffed the air with interest. "Where do we start?"

Dom sighed. "I have no clue. If my dad hid the Krugerrand, it could be anywhere."

"No safe or anything obvious, huh?" She tried to smile to break the tension.

"No. Although—" Dom stopped mid-sentence, turned, and walked through the connecting door to what she assumed was a large garage. He didn't wait for her, letting the door close loudly behind him.

Kendra glanced down at Smoky, who was still sniffing the air. Then the dog trotted over to the connecting door, sniffing along the baseboard. Her K9 sat and barked.

Kendra's blood turned to ice. She pulled her weapon and wrenched the door open. Dom didn't seem to notice, but looking beyond him, she saw a dark shadow moving along the back of what she now realized was a large plane hangar. It looked very similar to the one Jessica's husband, Logan, had built on the ranch. "Get down!"

At her command, Dom dropped to the ground just as Levy turned and fired wildly in their direction. He held something under his arm. What, Kendra couldn't tell. She fired three shots, one after the other, the way her oldest brother, Chase, had taught her.

Levy howled and hit the ground, dropping the box he held under his arm and his weapon.

Kendra rushed forward, kicking the gun away from Levy's outstretched hand. The box split open, revealing a spilled pile of gold coins. Then she noticed the blood pooling beneath Levy's body. Swallowing hard at the thought she may have killed a man, she lowered herself to one knee, feeling for a pulse. Levy was alive. For the moment.

Dom dropped beside the marshal, pulling the edges of Levy's coat together as a pressure dressing. "Go get help. I should have waited to see if Smoky would alert."

"Yeah, you should have." Before she could pull out the disposable phone Justin had given her, she heard a car engine. Fearing Levy had Bartoli with him, she jumped up and headed to the side door. When she saw Raine and Justin, she relaxed. Pushing open the door, she gestured for them to come in. "Levy's down. We need an ambulance."

Justin glared at her as Raine made the call. But she ignored her brother's annoyance.

This time, the danger was over for good.

"You should have waited for us." Anger flashed in Justin's eyes. "I called several times. What if Levy had shot you both? Then what?"

"Then I'd be in heaven with Mom and Dad." Kendra glanced over to where Raine was helping Dom stabilize Levy. "I'm sorry I didn't answer. I assumed Levy was in Canada by now."

"That's what happens when you're ruled by greed." Justin didn't look the least bit upset at how Levy clung to life. Then he sighed. "We should try to help save him. We may need him to find Bartoli."

It didn't take long for the Billings police and ambulance crew to arrive. The paramedics went to work on Levy, whisking him away within fifteen minutes. Despite everything, Kendra prayed Levy would survive. Her brother was right that they'd need him to get Bartoli.

Dom washed the blood from his hands, then knelt beside the box of Krugerrand. "I'm not sure how Levy found this."

"He used this." Kendra lifted a metal pole with a flat head on one end. "It's a metal detector."

Dom shook his head. "If they'd have just found the coins right away, they would have gotten away with it. Instead, they came at me like a bull charging a red flag."

"There was still Ramsey's confession," Kendra pointed out.

"Besides, nobody said criminals were smart," Raine said with a shrug.

Dom stood, leaving the coins on the floor of the hangar. "Take them. I don't want anything to do with stolen Krugerrand."

Kendra reached for his arm. This time, he didn't shake her off. Instead, he turned and folded her close. She clung to him, wishing things were different.

"They're not worth your life," Dom whispered in her ear. "Nothing is worth risking your life or that of your family."

"I feel the same way about you." She hugged him tight, then craned her head back to look up at him. "You're safe now. We all are."

He shook his head. "Not if Bartoli is still out there looking for the coins."

"We'll make an announcement that we found them," Raine said. "Besides, I think we can convince Jake and Jennifer to cooperate. That alone should help put Bartoli behind bars."

"Not if Levy hired them." Dom's expression appeared carved in stone. "I'm ready to go into witness protection, Raine. If that's the only way to keep Kendra and the rest of you safe, then I'm ready."

Kendra's heart squeezed painfully. "No, Dom. That's not necessary . . ."

He broke away from her embrace. "I won't risk you, Kendra. I won't! I love you!"

Her jaw dropped in shocked surprise. This was not exactly how she'd wanted to hear those three words. "I love you too! So you're not going away, understand?" She narrowed her gaze. "We'll figure this out, together."

Dom threw up his hands. "I give up." He jabbed a finger at Justin. "Talk some sense into your sister, would you?" With that, he strode into the house.

Justin took a step toward her, but Kendra lifted a hand. "Don't even try." She turned and followed Dominic inside. Smoky stayed close at her side.

Dom stood in the center of the room holding his head in his hands as if it might fall off if he let go. She crossed over to him. "I love you. I'm not leaving you." He opened his mouth to argue, but she kept going, "And if you're going into witness protection, then I am too."

He let out a harsh laugh. "Nice try, Kendra. You'd never leave your family."

"I don't want to leave them, but I love you. You, Dominic." She jabbed him in the chest with her index finger. "I love you! I don't want to live my life without you. So if you're going, then so am I." She glanced at Smoky. "But I don't think we can take Smoky with us. She's too noticcable."

"You can't leave your dog and your family. I won't let you do this." Dom's voice rose in agitation. "Please, Kendra, don't do this."

"That's up to you." She held his gaze. "I told you from the beginning we're in this together. Our parents died on that plane through no fault of their own. Their deaths have tied us together, Dom. Don't you see? God brought us together to learn the truth. And now that I've found the love I've envied amongst all my siblings, I'm not going to let you go."

"Kendra." His voice was a mere whisper, but

then he reached out and hauled her into his arms. "I don't deserve you."

Relief washed over her as she held him close. "You deserve my love the way I deserve yours."

"I love you so much." He pressed a kiss to her temple, then leaned back to lift her chin with his fingertip. His kiss was sweet at first, then turned molten hot. Kendra lost herself in his embrace until Smoky bumped her head against Kendra's thigh.

"Not now," she murmured, nudging the dog aside. Then she hauled Dom down for another kiss.

"Kendra? The police want to talk to you and Dom." Raine's wry tone broke them apart.

She swallowed a sigh of frustration. Couldn't they just have five minutes alone? But then Dom nodded and stepped back. "Of course."

Ignoring Raine's arched brow, Kendra led the way back to the hangar. Dom's home office was in the corner of the building. She headed that way, belatedly realizing this was the direction Levy had come from when she'd fired at him.

A rather skimpy Christmas tree stood in the far corner of the room, but what caught her attention was a perfectly square hole in the drywall at about the level of her face. "Is that where the coins were? I'm surprised the metal detector picked them up."

"Why wouldn't it? There are at least a hundred

coins, maybe more," Justin said with a shrug. "They were tucked behind a painting of Dom's father's plane. Not exactly an original hiding spot."

"So obvious I missed it," Dom muttered. "Although that picture is what made me head out here in the first place. I finally realized that if my father had hidden something, it might be behind the plane picture he loved."

"Don't beat yourself up for not realizing that sooner." Kendra took his hand in hers.

"He should have left me a clue." Dom gestured to the painting. "The picture was important to my father, so I left it undisturbed."

"Maybe your father assumed you'd look behind it. Or take it down," Justin said. "Although it's probably better you didn't, or you'd have ended up dead in a car crash like Helen Gingrass."

"It all worked out the way it was supposed to, I guess." Dom tugged her close. "Thanks to you, Kendra. And Smoky. If you hadn't jumped into the SUV at the last minute . . ."

"I'm glad I did." She sighed at Justin's glare. "And I'm glad you and Raine followed us."

"We need to take your statements." A Billings police officer gestured for her and Dominic to follow him outside. "And this is a crime scene. You can't stay here."

"That's okay, Dom will be staying with us at the Sullivan K9 Search and Rescue Ranch." She glanced over at him. "Right?"

He nodded slowly. "If your family agrees. If not, I'll find somewhere else . . ."

"You're staying." Kendra wasn't going to let Dom stay by himself. Not when Bartoli was still out there somewhere. "We'll be safe at the ranch until this is over."

"Hold on, Kendra," Justin protested. "Let's not forget about our pregnant sisters and the kids, Eli and Ben."

He was right. She had momentarily forgotten. "Okay, we'll find a place to stay. Maybe Griff can arrange another safe house. One that will actually keep us safe."

The next hour dragged by slowly. Kendra and Dom were separated and asked to provide their version of events independently of the other. When that was finished, she joined Dom, Raine, and Justin. The two dogs, Smoky and Stone, had played in the snow, wearing themselves out to the point they were both stretched out in the back crate areas of both SUVs sound asleep.

"I think we should stay in Billings," Kendra said to Dom as he handed Justin's key fob back. In return, Raine gave Kendra hers. "There are more hotels there than in all of Cody and Greybull combined."

"No need, you're coming to the ranch. I've cleared it with Chase." Justin grinned. "Although he wants to have a talk with Dominic once we get there."

"I understand. He has every right to be angry. It's my fault Kendra was in danger, and that you were hurt," Dom said.

"We'll talk to him together." Kendra gripped Dom's hand. "Don't worry, he'll be fine."

"Meet you there." Raine and Justin climbed into their SUV and drove off.

Kendra stepped closer to Dom. "Are you sure about this?"

"I'm sure I love you." He cupped her cheek with his hand and gave her a quick kiss. "Let's not keep your brother waiting, though. I'm already starting off on the wrong foot with your family. I'd hate to make it worse than it already is."

"They'll love you because I love you." She kissed him, then pressed the key fob into his hand. "Trust me."

"I do." Dom held her gaze for a long moment, then slid in behind the wheel. Kendra glanced up as large flakes of snow began to fall. One good thing about living in Wyoming, they always had a white Christmas.

She couldn't wait to spend the holiday with Dom and her family. Even with their uncertain future, her heart filled with hope as they made the trip back home.

EPILOGUE

Christmas Eve

Dom stood off to the side of the large gathering space in the main lodge of the ranch. Not to be antisocial, he just wasn't sure he'd ever get used to being a part of the huge Sullivan family. There were so many of them! Not just Kendra's eight older siblings and their spouses, but also Doug's sister, Emily, and her husband, Owen. There was even another guy named Miles, who was Bailey's brother who had been invited to the holiday gathering. Dom had all their names memorized now, but a simple family meal was still total chaos.

Especially when you added the eleven dogs and three kids to the mix.

After his initial tense meeting with Chase three weeks ago, their relationship had gotten better.

Kendra was right, her siblings and their respective spouses and kids welcomed him into the fold as if he were one of them.

And in a way, he supposed he was. Or soon would be.

The ring burned a hole in his pocket. He thought it would be the perfect Christmas gift for Kendra, but now that the time had come, he was nervous.

"Relax," Griff said as he came to stand beside him. "I just got a call from my boss. Jake and Jennifer admitted to their part in shooting at you and Kendra and killing Helen Gingrass. Thanks to Levy's cooperation, they found and arrested Bartoli. Levy had apparently wanted to spend his retirement in the lap of luxury, which was why he'd gotten involved. The Krugerrand has been returned to South Africa. The danger is over for good."

"Yeah," Doug agreed, coming up to stand on his other side. "You don't have to worry about going into WITSEC now."

"I have a feeling the Sullivans wouldn't have allowed me to do that anyway," Dom admitted with a smile. "Not after Kendra threatened to go with me."

"True." Griff grinned. "They're an interesting bunch, aren't they?"

"That's an understatement." Logan slapped

Dom on the back as he joined them. "Takes a strong man to marry a Sullivan woman."

Dom arched a brow. "How did you know I'm planning to propose?"

"We've all been there." Doug smiled as his gaze landed on his very pregnant wife. "And we're here to support you, Dom, in any way we can. Us non-Sullivan guys need to stick together."

"Yep." Griff elbowed him in the ribs. "You're going to want to make your move soon, though. While the kids are preoccupied with the dogs for the moment."

Dom appreciated their camaraderie. He'd quit his job and was interviewing for a different job with the FBI based on Griff's urging. He planned to put his house and hangar up for sale after the first of the year. He liked living on the ranch. Maybe being a part of the family wasn't such a bad thing after all. Chase had given his blessing, so that was a good start.

He pushed away from the wall, crossed the room, and snagged Kendra's arm. Then he turned to the group. "If I could have a moment?"

Everyone was still talking, so Doug Bridges whistled loudly between his fingers. Instantly, a hush came over the room. Doug nodded encouragingly. "Go on, Dom."

Drawing a deep breath, Dom turned to Kendra

and dropped to one knee. "Kendra, I love you. Will you please do me the honor of marrying me?"

"Really? Are you sure?" Kendra searched his gaze as if half expecting him to bolt. "Maybe we should wait . . ."

His heart sank. Was she having second thoughts? "I love you. I want to marry you. But if you need more time . . ."

"It's not that," Kendra said quickly. "We've only known each other a few months. I thought you'd want more time."

The tight band around his heart eased. "I'm ready. If you are. Please marry me?"

"Uh, Kendra? You'd better hurry and say yes." Maya stood and waddled toward them. "Baby Boy Bridges is about to be born."

"Wait, what?" Doug paled. "That's not possible. We just saw the doctor yesterday. He said it would be a few days yet, up to a week!"

"He's wrong." Maya winced as her belly tightened with a contraction. "Trust me. We're having a Christmas baby. Luke Bridges will be born tonight or tomorrow morning."

Dom stayed focused on Kendra as everyone else turned their attention toward Maya and Doug. Talk about being upstaged. He held her gaze, waiting for her answer.

"Yes, Dominic. Yes, I absolutely want to marry

you." Kendra smiled, wiped a tear from her eye, then tugged him up to his feet. She threw her arms around his neck and drew him down for a kiss. Behind her, Doug continued babbling about how the baby shouldn't be coming so soon. "I hope you know what you're getting yourself into," she whispered, before capturing his mouth with hers in a deep kiss.

As her family burst into applause, cheering them on, Doug and Maya hustled toward the door. The loud cheers gave him an inkling of what she meant. There was no privacy with this bunch, that was for sure.

But if the other guys who'd been brave enough to marry Sullivan women could do it, so could he.

Because love and family were all that mattered.

THANKS so much for reading *Scent of Murder*, the last book in my Sullivan K9 Search and Rescue series! I hope you enjoyed these stories as much as I had fun writing them. And if you're sad this series is over, fear not! I'm kicking off a new series next year. If you're ready to read Grady McFarland's story in *Deadly Abduction*, the first book in my Grayson's Guardians series, click here!

DEAR READER

Thanks for reading *Scent of Murder*! I hope you enjoyed Kendra and Dominic's story. I've had fun writing about the Sullivan siblings. While I'm sad the series has come to an end, I'm already working on my next series! The first book in my Grayson's Guardians series, *Deadly Abduction*, will be available next year! I never formally introduced you to Joel's high school friend Grady McFarland, but you'll meet him soon enough. I hope you give my new series a try.

Don't forget, you can purchase ebooks or audiobooks directly from my website and will receive a 15% discount by using the code **LauraScott15**.

I adore hearing from my readers! I can be found through my website at https://www.laurascottbook s.com, via Facebook at https://www.facebook.com/

LauraScottBooks, Instagram at https://www.insta gram.com/laurascottbooks/, and X at https://x.com/ laurascottbooks. Please take a moment to subscribe to my YouTube channel at youtube.com/@LauraS-cottBooks-wr1xl?sub_confirmation=1. Also take a moment to sign up for my monthly newsletter to learn about my new book releases! All subscribers receive a free novella not available for purchase on any platform.

Until next time,

Laura Scott

PS. Keep reading for a sneak peek of *Deadly Abduction*...

DEADLY ABDUCTION

Chapter One

Grady "Mac" McFarland stared at his boss, Rex Grayson. Normally, he gave his former army captain a lot of respect, but Rex seemed to have gone off the deep end this time. This mission was unlike any of the others Grayson's Guardians had sent him on. "You really want me to be a bodyguard for a rich woman and her seven-year-old kid?"

Rex nodded. The captain was only four years older than Grady's thirty-two, but the grim weariness in his boss's gray eyes betrayed the emotional toil they'd suffered during their last tour in Iraq. Grady, he was only Mac to his army buddies, knew that Rex had taken the loss of their teammates hard and that he'd ended up getting divorced after he'd returned stateside. From what Grady could tell, the guy was still grieving the loss. "Yeah, that's exactly what Ms. Lauren Chandler is asking and paying us for. I really need you to do this."

"Why me?" The question popped out before he could stop it. The truth was someone from the team had to take this assignment. They were usually sent on rescue missions of some sort or another. None of them were experts on keeping an eye on a socialite and her daughter.

"Because you have good instincts and investigative skills." When his phone dinged, Rex reached for it. "Ms. Chandler has some strong opinions on who she'll accept as her bodyguard. Besides, I have a feeling that we're going to need to work with the police and the FBI on this." Rex held up his phone. "She's here."

Grady swallowed a groan as he rose to his feet. The door to the office swung open revealing a beautiful blonde wearing a long leather coat that probably cost more than his house back in Cody, Wyoming. Lauren Chandler looked rich, even without the sparkly diamond studs in her ears and expensive looking clothes. She had a large leather handbag slung over her shoulder. She looked to be roughly his age, he thought. Her pale skin indicated she didn't get out in the sun much, or maybe it was just that it was early February. The young girl beside her had long brown hair that was held back from her face with a pink headband, and she had the same brilliant blue eyes as her mother. She also wore a thick navy-blue parka in deference to the freezing cold Chicago temperatures.

Not unlike Wyoming, he thought with a sigh. No such luck he'd be sent to Florida or some other southern state in the winter.

"Ms. Chandler, this is Mac, er, Grady McFarland. Mac, this is Ms. Lauren Chandler and her daughter, Lucy."

"Nice to meet you." He forced a smile on his face as he stepped forward to offer his hand. To his surprise, Lauren had a firm grip.

"Thanks for agreeing to help me." She glanced at her daughter, and amended, "Help us."

"I was just about to fill Mac in on what's been happening." Rex gestured to the chairs beside his. "Please have a seat."

Lauren removed her leather bag and dropped gracefully into the chair beside his. Her daughter took the seat on her other side. It was almost as if Lauren had purposefully put herself between him and Lucy.

"A seven-year-old girl was abducted two days ago," Rex said, breaking the silence. "Her name is Ariel Turner, and she happens to be one of Lucy's closest friends. They attend the same private school together."

Grady frowned. "And Ms. Chandler believes that abduction is an indication Lucy is also in danger?" In his mind, that was a leap, even if Lucy's parents were rich.

"Please, call me Lauren. I have video on my laptop." She surprised him by removing a computer from her large bag and opening it. "I think when you see this, you'll understand my concern."

Rex inclined his head, indicating she should go ahead with the video. Grady leaned over to see the screen as Lauren queued it up. A whiff of her perfume teased his senses, but he ignored it. As a client, Lauren was off-limits, even if she wasn't rich and had a daughter. *Three strikes you're out*, he thought wryly. Besides, he wasn't interested in dating anyone after his former fiancée broke things off. His job caused him to travel across the US, and frankly, he liked the different missions Rex Grayson assigned to them. *Until this most recent request*, he silently admitted.

Beside him, Lauren expanded the video on the screen and hit the play button. A young girl wearing a navy-blue parka and a pink headband walked down the sidewalk. She wore white tights beneath a navy-blue and green plaid pleated skirt. At first, he thought the girl was Lucy, as they both had brown hair and the same headband, but as he searched the girl's facial features, he realized it wasn't.

A man wearing a ski mask suddenly appeared on the screen. He swooped the girl into his arms and darted away. The kidnapping happened so fast, Mac blinked in surprise when the short video ended.

"What in the world?" He glanced at Lauren. "Do the police have any leads on who did this? Is there more video that shows the vehicle the kidnapper used to escape?"

"No." Her expression was strained. "The most interesting thing is that Ariel was released less than three hours later." She paused, then added, "After the kidnappers realized they'd grabbed the wrong girl."

A chill snaked down his spine. Okay, now he understood. He caught a glimpse of Lucy's concerned face and framed his comment as carefully as possible. "You believe your daughter is in danger."

Lauren's blue eyes flashed. "I know she is."

"Ariel was scared." Lucy's voice was small. "But the bad man didn't hurt her."

Mac's throat tightened at the thought of Lucy being snatched the same way Ariel had been. He sat up straighter, accepting the gravity of the situation. "Do Ariel and Lucy always dress alike? I mean, other than wearing their school uniform."

Lauren nodded. "They like to pretend to be twins." Her brow furrowed. "Although not anymore."

"Ariel's mother doesn't like me." Lucy's blue eyes were bright with tears. "She said we can't play together anymore."

"It's okay, Lucy." Lauren wrapped her arm around her daughter's slim shoulders, hugging her close. "Ms. Turner is just upset about what happened. I'm sure that once the bad man is behind bars, everything will go back to normal."

"I hope so." Lucy's voice was muffled against her mother's coat. "Ariel is my best friend."

"I know, sweetie." Lauren's stricken gaze turned to Mac's. "Lucy needs protection. And we also need to understand the source of the threat."

Grady glanced at Rex, then slowly nodded. "I'm sure the local police and the FBI are working on that as well."

"They are, but not with the sense of urgency I expect." Lauren's blue eyes glittered with anger. "Ariel being released has lulled them into complacency. They aren't taking the threat as seriously as I'd like."

He arched a brow at that. When Rex didn't say anything, he nodded. "Okay, let's start with who might have a grudge against you."

Lauren glanced at Lucy, then back at him. "I'd be happy to discuss this at length when we get home."

Grady almost argued, but then he realized Lauren didn't want to go into details in front of her daughter. With a resigned sigh, he nodded. "Fine. What's your address? I can meet you there."

She arched a brow. "I'm not leaving without you. My driver dropped us off and escorted us up to the tenth floor. From here, I expect you'll be handling all aspects of our transportation."

So she expected him to be her chauffeur. Great. He did his best to hide his annoyance. "I'm driving a Jeep, not a limo."

"I didn't expect a limo." Her tone held a note of disdain. "And there's one more thing we need to discuss."

He glanced again at Rex, who grimaced as if he knew what was coming. He braced himself for the worst. Did she expect him to wear some sort of chauffeur's uniform? Or some other uniform to make sure he blended into the background when she did—whatever socialites did?

"I need you to pretend to be my fiancé." Lauren turned to face him. "I don't want the world to know my daughter is in danger."

He blinked. That was so not what he'd expected. "Your fiancé?"

"Yes." A faint blush stained her cheeks. "From

what I understand, you're not involved with anyone, correct?" When he managed to nod in agreement, she went on. "Then there's no reason the public in general won't buy our story."

"Except for the fact that we've only seen each other for the first time today," he drawled. Or the fact that he was a former army sergeant from Cody, Wyoming, about as far from the high society page as you could get.

Annoyance flashed in her eyes as she glanced toward Rex. His boss cleared his throat. "Mac, er, Grady will gladly take on the role of your fiancé to keep you and your daughter safe."

He would? Swallowing a flash of irritation, he forced a nod. "Of course. Whatever you think is best."

"Thank you." Satisfied with the arrangement, Lauren rose. She dug a check from her handbag, which doubled as a computer case, and set it on Rex's desk. "For the first week as agreed. I'm hoping you, Grady, and the police are able to figure out who is responsible for abducting Ariel by then."

"Thank you." Rex glanced at the check, then rose. He held out his hand. "Mac, er, Grady will protect you and your daughter with his life."

"I'm counting on it." Lauren's expression was grim as she shook Rex's hand, then turned to him. "Would you like to be called Grady or Mac?"

He cleared his throat. "Grady is fine. It's only my army buddies that call me Mac."

"Fine." She nodded briskly. "Let's go then." She placed her computer in her bag and was about to sling it over her shoulder when he held out his hand. It took a moment for her to realize he intended to carry it for her. "It looks like a purse," she said, flustered by his action.

"That's okay." He shrugged into his leather bomber jacket and took the bag from her hand. "I've got it."

"Thank you." She turned to her daughter. "Let's go, Lucy."

As he followed Lauren and Lucy out of the office, he turned to shoot one last look at Rex. He wasn't the only single agent Rex had working for him. They were all single, although Micah was seeing someone last Grady had heard.

The only reason he was going along with this pretend fiancé/bodyguard deal was the image of the masked man snatching Ariel off the street in broad daylight and knowing Lucy was the intended target.

Rex was right about one thing. He'd protect Lucy and her mother with his life if necessary.

LAUREN GLANCED FURTIVELY over her shoulder as she stepped out of the office building into the bright sunshine. Her face felt like it might crack from her forced smile. Every nerve ending was on high alert for a masked man to pop out of the shadows at any moment.

She hadn't slept in the two days since Ariel had been abducted by mistake. And even with hiring a bodyguard, she couldn't relax. One man could only do so much. She'd been tempted to hire a team of bodyguards, but that would only advertise the danger.

"Stay a few feet in front of me." Grady's low, husky voice had her glancing at him. Then she just as quickly looked away. He was tall, broad-shouldered, and incredibly handsome, if you liked rugged-looking men.

Which to her dismay, her long-dormant hormones did.

Grady put his arm around her waist, keeping her positioned to his left. She kept Lucy close, then stiffened when she realized Grady held a gun in his right hand.

Well, what did you think? she mentally chided herself. Of course, her bodyguard would be armed with a weapon.

"You're supposed to be my fiancé," she whispered

as he directed her to his car. He'd said he drove a Jeep, but somehow she'd expected something with a rag top that he'd use to go four-wheeling in the mountains, not a brand-new Jeep Grand Wagoneer.

"Yeah, but this fiancé plans to be ready for anything." He hustled her to the passenger-side door. "Does Lucy need a booster seat?"

"Technically, yes, but for now, she'll be fine." The booster seat was the least of her worries, although she was a little surprised he'd mentioned it. Most single guys were clueless about that kind of thing. Unless Grady had kids? Whatever. It didn't matter as long as he did his job.

Except it did matter if he was going to put his life on the line for her. She waited for Lucy to get settled in the back seat before climbing in herself. When Grady slid in behind the wheel, she asked, "Do you have kids?"

"What? No." He looked startled by her question. "Why do you ask?"

"I—was surprised you knew about booster seats."

"I may have grown up in small-town Wyoming, but I didn't live under a rock." His western drawl was back. "I'm friends with a guy who has eight siblings. I'm familiar with what it's like to be around kids."

"I see." She flushed. "I didn't mean any dis-respect."

"None taken." He said the words easily, but she sensed his annoyance. She closed her eyes and tried to calm her racing heart. There was no reason to care what Grady McFarland thought about her. He was her bodyguard and fake fiancé. Once this nightmare was over, she'd never see him again.

As he waited for a break in the traffic, she twisted in her seat to look behind them. She hadn't seen anyone suspicious following her and Lucy, but that didn't mean someone wasn't lurking back there, waiting for the opportunity to make his move. The truth was, she had no idea who would want to kidnap Lucy.

The motive had to be money because that was the only thing that made sense. She hadn't mentioned how she'd been kidnapped once as a child after her father had made the news as the first Chicago billionaire. Granted, that was twenty-five years ago, when she was about Lucy's age.

That her daughter would be targeted in the same way bothered her. She'd cooperated with the investigation and had racked her brain for a list of suspects. But as far as she could tell, the police were no closer to finding this guy.

Which did not bode well for Lucy.

"I'll need your address," Grady said, interrupting her thoughts.

She rattled off the building number, then gestured to the skyscraper looming to the right. It looked closer than it actually was. "It's the black building behind that one, it's called Savion Enterprises. We live in the penthouse apartment."

"Underground parking I presume?" He glanced at her.

"Yes." She wasn't sure why Grady made her feel nervous. If anything, it should have been the other way around. She was born and raised here in the Windy City, but he was a fish out of water. Or he should have been, except that he carried himself with an air of confidence that she envied.

Then again, his child wasn't the intended target of a ransom demand. She and Lucy were just another job for him. Her father had recommended Grayson's Guardians when she'd asked him for advice. Apparently, Rex Grayson was some sort of war hero who had led a team in combat who all earned bronze stars for their bravery under fire.

She'd jumped at the opportunity of having someone with battle experience protecting her daughter. Now that she was sitting there beside Grady, doubts pummeled her.

He looked competent enough, but she hadn't

anticipated his being so—big. Muscular. Rugged. Strong.

She put a hand to her throbbing temple and told herself to stop being ridiculous. Her lack of sleep was getting to her.

"Are you hungry?" Grady's question caught her by surprise. "I'm happy to stop and grab something if you'd like."

"No thanks. Clara, our housekeeper, probably has dinner cooking by now."

"Okay." If he was surprised to hear she had a housekeeper, he didn't show it. "Do you know anything else about the vehicle used in the abduction?"

"The car was a black SUV." His Jeep was black too. "I believe it was a Honda."

His green gaze flicked to the rearview mirror, then back at her. "Lots of black SUVs on the road."

Her heart thumped painfully against her sternum. She twisted in her seat again to look through the back window. "Do you see something suspicious?"

"Just stating a fact." His calm demeanor did not make her feel any better. "Traffic is so congested here that it's hard to spot a tail. That's why I was thinking it would be good to stop and get food. See if the two black SUVs behind us stick around or keep going."

"Mom? Is the bad man back there?" The fear

underscoring Lucy's tone wrenched at her heart. No child should be afraid of being kidnapped.

"I don't think so, sweetie. Mr.—uh, Grady is just being cautious." She flashed him a pointed look. "Right?"

"Right." Grady made eye contact with her daughter. "Don't worry. Nothing bad is going to happen while I'm around, okay?"

"Okay." Lucy's tremulous smile tugged at her heart. Having divorced Nelson five years ago, obtaining sole custody of Lucy, her daughter didn't have any memories of him. Since Nelson was in jail for manslaughter, Lauren preferred to keep it that way. How she'd been blind to Nelson's true nature, she had no idea.

Maybe it was wrong to be glad Nelson was in jail. Their divorce had been contentious despite the prenup she'd required him to sign. She'd soon learned he'd only married her for her money.

Whatever. That was old news. As much as she could easily envision Nelson doing something as low as abducting his own daughter for a hefty ransom, he was dead.

Someone else was behind this. Too bad the list of suspects pretty much included everyone who resented the wealthy.

"I changed my mind. Let's stop for pizza." Once the idea took hold in her mind, she couldn't let it go.

She glanced at Grady. "You can have whatever you like, but we need to order one pepperoni pizza for Lucy."

"Really? Pepperoni pizza?" Lucy sounded excited. "Yay!"

A reluctant smile tugged at the corner of her mouth as she glanced back at her daughter. "We'll have to blame Grady for wanting pizza so Clara doesn't get upset with us."

"Oh yeah?" Grady's drawl made her glance at him to see if he was truly upset. The twinkle in his eyes indicated he wasn't. "Sure, make me the bad guy right out of the gate."

"It's just that she fusses over us and takes it personally when we don't eat what she's prepared." Lauren shrugged. "Normally, that's not a problem as I prefer to serve Lucy healthy meals."

"Healthy is fine, but this is a special occasion," Grady said. When she frowned in confusion, he rolled his eyes. "Our engagement! Surely you haven't forgotten our engagement already."

She blushed at his teasing. The people around her tended to cater to whatever she wanted. Which, quite frankly, got old fast. She wasn't used to being teased.

"Of course, I didn't forget. That's a great excuse for us to use." She decided not to point out that if they were truly engaged, they'd be celebrating with steak, lobster, and champagne. For a moment, she envied Grady's simpler lifestyle. Then she gave herself a mental shake. There was no point in wishing for something else. She'd been given many blessings. And she'd made it her mission to champion various charity events. Her favorite by far was the work she did as the spokesperson for Saint Mary's Children's Hospital in Chicago. Lucy had needed emergency open heart surgery when she was born. From that point forward, Lauren had made it her mission to make sure all children received the care they needed, regardless of their ability to pay.

Thankfully, she was in a position to make that happen. Not only were her parents wealthy, but her father's parents had also left her a large trust fund. A fund that Nelson had tried to get his hands on.

The jerk.

"What's your favorite pizza?" Grady asked, interrupting her thoughts.

"Um." She didn't want to admit that when they ordered pizza, Clara took care of the details.

"I like Captain Jack's pizza," Lucy announced. "That's the kind Ariel's parents get from the store."

Grady shot her a quizzical look, probably wondering what kind of world her daughter lived in. "Any pizza you think looks good is fine with us," she hastily added.

"Got it." He made an abrupt turn to the right.

She braced herself with a hand on the dashboard when she heard a loud crack.

Confused, she looked around, wondering if someone had gotten in a car crash.

"Down!" Grady shoved her head down as he drove the Jeep up and over a curb. The jarring motion made her teeth snap together.

"Mommy?" Lucy's plaintive voice had her turning to look at her daughter. When she noticed the rear window was shattered, she belatedly realized the sound wasn't a car crash.

It had been gunfire!